The Quick

Also by Laura Spinney

The Doctor

The Quick

LAURA SPINNEY

FOURTH ESTATE • *London*

First published in Great Britain in 2007 by
Fourth Estate
An imprint of HarperCollins*Publishers*
77–85 Fulham Palace Road
London W6 8JB
www.4thestate.co.uk

1

A catalogue record for this book is available from the British Library

ISBN-13 978-0-00-724050-0
ISBN-10 0-00-724050-3

Set in Minion by Palimpsest Book Production Ltd, Grangemouth, Stirlingshire

Printed in Great Britain by Clays Ltd, St Ives plc

This book is proudly printed on paper which contains wood from well managed forests, certified in accordance with the rules of the Forest Stewardship Council.
For more information about FSC,
please visit www.fsc.uk.org

FSC
Mixed Sources
Product group from well-managed forests and other controlled sources
www.fsc.org Cert no. TT-COC-2139
© 1996 Forest Stewardship Council

For Richard

1

Patient DL had already been in the hospital ten years before I discovered her. She occupied a small room at the end of a corridor on the top floor, forgotten by all except her visitors and the staff who cared for her. There had been no change in her condition in a decade, no deterioration towards death nor stirring of life. It was a sad case, because she was quite a young woman, and it was the opinion of her doctors that she would remain that way until her natural death, or until someone put an end to her life – whichever happened first.

I arrived at the hospital seven years after DL. I brought with me quite a reputation, and by the time I took up my post it was understood that I would see only the most difficult cases. It was therefore only a matter of time before I came across her, she who was to become my obsession, the most tantalising and elusive of my patients. She had already been there so long she was considered a part of the fabric of the place, as essential to it as the lift shafts, operating theatres and incinerators. It was as if Patient DL, or someone like her, had always occupied that small room at the end of the corridor on the fifth floor.

Sooner or later, then, I would find my way to her. And yet for three long years I managed to avoid it. No whisper of her ever reached me, even though I must have passed people in the corridors, or nodded to them in the lifts, who had seen her with their own eyes. How could that be? I can't explain, except to say that in some strange way, I feel it could only have happened *in that place.*

After DL entered the hospital, the city underwent a period of rapid change. It was the first decade of a new millennium, some said the dawn of a new enlightenment, and the politicians were in empire-building mood. They gave the architects free rein, and the architects played with the skyline like plasticine. Their techniques and materials had advanced to such a level that they could afford to have a little fun at last. I would glance upwards and laugh – I admired their playfulness. But the hospital was older, more earthbound. It wasn't designed to draw attention to itself, but to shelter, or to hide, the most fragile of our brethren. It squatted at the heart of this giddy, gaudy construction site, like a trapdoor you might stumble through by chance.

Everybody knew about that grand old hospital, with its historic reputation: backdrop to some of the greatest discoveries in medicine. But ask them to point to it on a map, and they would shrug their shoulders and grin. It was all but invisible to the untrained eye, and this invisibility was only partly an accident of town planning. The front of the hospital, the tip of the iceberg, occupied one side of a pretty Georgian square which was reached by several cobbled alleyways. These narrow openings – just wide enough to admit an ambulance – were easy to miss. If you peered into them from the busy street outside, they looked dark and uninviting. So people carried on walking into the brightly lit theatre district, or in the other direction, to the museums and restaurants. They rarely came to the square without an appointment, unless they arrived by ambulance, or fell in drunk. And so it was cut off from the city that encircled and pressed in on it, like an eddy in a fast-flowing river.

On passing through one of the narrow alleyways, and emerging into this peaceful backwater, the newcomer would be presented with a red-brick, rather austere building, with a gabled roof and regimented rows of small windows. In fact, that façade was deceptive, because grey, military-style blocks stretched back for some distance behind it, fanning out in all directions. There was a wide entrance with a flight of shallow steps leading up to it, a long ramp for wheelchair users and an ambulance bay on the street. Nowhere on the front of the building would you find the word 'hospital', something the reader might find hard to believe, until I explain that it had no emergency department, and the administration wished to discourage the scourge of every casualty room – the hospital tourist – from dropping in. Even the ambulances that served it lacked the usual characteristic markings. So it was only when you entered the building, and sometimes not even then, that you realised what kind of a place you had come to.

What was that place? To those in the know, it was the country's leading authority on the treatment of brain disease. That was its reputation at the time I'm writing about, the beginning of the new millennium, but originally its purpose was to treat psychiatric patients – those suffering from disorders of the mind. The distinction has now largely lost its significance – the mind being considered a product of the brain, not able to exist separately from it – but the outdated ideas persisted in bricks and mortar, and many new visitors remarked, on gazing up at the façade, that the hospital had the look and feel of an asylum about it.

The unhappy illusion persisted when you stepped inside. The architect had followed his instructions to the letter, and his instructions a century or more back were that patients were more likely to recover if they were only exposed to others with the same flavour of insanity as themselves. It gave their universe some coherence, the thinking went. So as soon as you passed through the grand portal you found yourself in a large, echoing hall, with the feel of a railway station about it. In the middle, a white-painted signpost pointed into the mouths of three wide corridors, exacerbating the feeling that you were embarking on a journey, destination unknown. The children were led off to the west wing, the elderly to the east; everyone else straight on, to the north.

The north wing was much bigger than the other two. It consisted of a solid, five-storey block built around a rectangle of garden. The first three floors housed the administrative offices, consulting rooms and operating theatres; the top two, the wards. These were divided up again, according to whether the patients were surgical or non-surgical, public or private. A colour-coding system told you which sector you were in at any time. The top floor was reserved for the long-term, gravely ill.

This north wing was the place I dreamed of graduating to during the years after I completed my training, years I spent in a series of provincial hospitals. Finally, the longed-for invitation came and I took up residence there. I was given a suite of rooms on the second floor, and a couple of assistants to deal with the run-of-the-mill cases – the dementias, common aphasias and so forth. Patients were brought down to my rooms from the wards, in wheelchairs or leaning on sticks, and my assistants would sit them down and, with smiles and encouraging nods, ask them to name a picture of a French horn or a microscope. If the patient was bedridden, or prone to lapses in consciousness, one of them would ride up in the lift and perform the tests at the bedside. Meanwhile, I devoted my attention to conditions so rare a specialist would be lucky to come across one in his lifetime. Often I never laid eyes on the patient. Doctors sent me meticulous descriptions from hospitals I hadn't heard of, in countries I'd never visited. I would pass happy hours, my window open on to the garden, which smelt wonderfully of daffodils in spring, and roses in summer, devising new ways of probing their inner life. New tasks to set them, new games to play.

The essential problem for me, always, was to get past the patient's diminished ability to communicate, to see what was preserved behind – like tapping a wall until it gave back a hollow ring, then stripping away layers of wallpaper to reveal the panelled door beneath. To ask, 'What seems to be the problem?', but not in words. I used line drawings, flashes of light, music. I might ask the patient to press a button when a certain sequence of numbers appeared, or the face of a famous person. With my help, the doctors in La Paz showed that the bullet that had robbed an Indian boy of speech, had also liberated a prodigious talent for long division. An old woman living on the shores of Lake Garda, supposedly struck dumb by a stroke, discovered that it was only Italian she had lost: if someone addressed her in her mother tongue, the Veronese dialect she had learned as a child and long since abandoned, she responded fluently, if with a rather limited, infantile vocabulary.

Those are well-known stories now, of course; the patients enjoy a certain notoriety, even make a modest living from their talents, or defects. They travel the world from laboratory to laboratory, willingly subjecting themselves to new and ever more elaborate attempts to probe the secrets of their brains. They have turned their idiosyncrasies to their advantage, and created a cottage industry. Meanwhile, new curiosities are born every day, in the pages of obscure journals, from where a select few of them will rise to neurological stardom.

My name would often be included among the authors of such a paper. My long list of publications, all of them in prestigious journals, earned me the right to organise my time as I saw fit, and not to have to venture too often above the second floor. On the rare occasions that I did, I was accompanied by a consultant, various other specialists and, of course, my two assistants. With this retinue making constant demands on my attention, asking my opinion on this or that, I had little opportunity to look to left or right. Blinkered as I was, I failed to notice the patient who lay three floors above my office, unable to move or speak, whose doctors considered beyond my help.

The Quick

In hindsight, it seems only right that Mezzanotte should have been the one to draw her to my attention, he who always knew where to look for the most interesting question, and then how to go about answering it.

2

That hospital, detached though it was from the city it served, represented my ideal of modern medicine. The people who ran it, the director and her deputies, didn't parade through the corridors inspecting the work in progress. They were discreet, in fact we never saw them, but their competence was evident in its smooth running. Patients always left better off than when they had entered, unless there was nothing that could be done for them, or unless they left via the crematorium chimney, which was the only other possible exit. Everything that happened happened for a reason, and being able to count myself among its several hundred employees, I admit, only added to my sense of its rightness.

I preferred to be in my office than in the small flat that had been provided for me nearby. I went home to sleep, to change my clothes and pick up my post. If I was obliged to wait around there in the day, to receive a delivery, say, or because it was Sunday, I quickly began to feel restless. I preferred to walk the short distance to the theatres, pick one at random and lose myself in a fictional world for a few hours.

But above all, I longed to be back in my office. It was a source of great pleasure to me to turn my chair to face the window, to see beyond it the facing side of the north wing, which enclosed our little garden.

My office was small, but comfortable. It was painted white, and there was room for the desk, a couple of armchairs and some bookshelves. On the wall by the door, in two symmetrical rows, were arranged the framed certificates which, with ribbons and seals, announced my membership of various professional organisations. I would have to step right up to the window to look down on the garden, on the mosaic of lawn, flower beds and paths lined with benches and ornamental fruit trees. But it was enough for me to know it was there. The paediatric and geriatric wings were too small to have gardens. But the north wing did, and that lent it a certain grandeur. It made it the spiritual heart of the hospital; its soul. More than that, the lighted windows on the third floor of the other side appealed to my liking for symmetry.

The reason was that those squares of frosted glass belonged to the operating theatres. Behind them, under the bright theatre lights, faceless surgeons in green overalls, caps and masks drilled through cranium, lifted flaps of bone and scooped out tumours. They inserted grafts, or probes, applied pulses of electricity, then retreated through tough, transparent curtains of membrane, stitching them up behind them as they went. They repaired the hardware, and after the patient had spent a little time recuperating on the wards, I would start the slow process of reprogramming it. I made good on their promises. Our efforts complemented each other entirely.

And so it went on. For three long years, between us, we sculpted the material at our disposal and sent it back into the world, to use the frightful jargon, in a more highly functioning state. There was no let-up in the work. As the recognised authority on every kind of brain disease, we were supplied by hospitals all over the country – those hospitals I had worked in previously, at earlier stages of my career – and even hospitals in Europe and further afield.

If there was ever a pause in my daily schedule, perhaps because a patient had failed to turn up for an appointment, or died in the night, I would lean back in my chair, close my eyes and let my mind wander. Often, in those rare, peaceful moments, I would think of Mezzanotte. We hadn't spoken since I had taken up my post (it was he who tipped me off, by telephone, before I received the official letter of invitation), but I felt his exacting, enquiring presence all around me. He was, in fact, less than a kilometre away as the crow flies, in a large, light office at the top of one of the architects' new follies – a rhomboid in glass and steel. From there, he commanded six hundred square metres of state-of-the-art laboratory and all those who laboured in it.

My debt to Mezzanotte was so great that it could never be repaid. I first went to work for him almost by chance. I simply answered an advertisement in one of our professional journals, not knowing who had placed it. At the time he was interested in the question of why we sleep, and hunting for clues among the human sleep anomalies: insomnia, narcolepsy, incubi or night terrors. But mainly insomnia. Even then, he ran a large group and I forget who it was who interviewed me. But I was accepted and my duties were explained to me. I was to interview the patients, note their symptoms and perform the various psychological tests. Last but not least, I had to make sure they understood they weren't being offered a cure.

For this task I was allocated one of the old teaching rooms in the university's Department of Anatomy, a few streets away from the hospital. It was lonely work, and back then I was still inexperienced. In my field, in the medical profession as a whole, you have to develop an immunity to human suffering or the first hard-luck story will pierce you through. But my outer casing hadn't sealed over yet and I quickly discovered what a lack of sleep could do to people. In the most extreme cases, it turned them into monsters. A procession of unravelled men and women trooped through my room, red-eyed and raw, and told me such tales of woe that at the end of every day I would break down in tears.

My contract lasted three months, and during that time I never once spoke to Mezzanotte or even stood in the same room as him. I saw him occasionally, from a distance, striding across a street, his head turned away from me. He wore an ivory silk scarf wound tightly round his neck, and his left hand was always tucked into his jacket pocket, as if he were concealing something there. I had seen his picture, of course, many times, though he was still some way off the height of his fame – not yet a household name. He was forty-five years old. A tall man, slightly stooped, he wore beautifully cut tweed jackets a little too long beyond their natural lifetime. In the olive-skinned oval of his face burned two dark, soulful eyes.

He had a high brow framed by thick brown curls, and soft, full lips. A passionate-looking Mediterranean, but reserved – some would say, cold as ice. The passion lay in the features he had been given, not in the way he used them. His face was curiously expressionless, and the general view in scientific circles, though it was only whispered, was that his brilliance hid a lack of human feeling – something I later found to be not quite accurate.

What I knew about the professor at that time necessarily came to me second-hand. He was born of mixed stock, of an aristocratic Italian father and a mother of unknown origin, possibly Hungarian. Mezzanotte spoke five languages, but understood or read several more; he was knowledgeable about sixteenth-century Italian art, and had built up his own collection of paintings which circulated on permanent loan, since he himself was of no fixed abode. By that I mean that he moved around the world, led by the latest question that obsessed him and the location of the tools and people he needed to answer it. He was at home anywhere in Europe and had lived happily in the Arizona desert too. He had left behind laboratories in Trieste, Copenhagen, Tucson and Tokyo, all of which continued to thrive, and his name had been mentioned in the same breath as the Nobel Prize – though back then, he had yet to win it.

He had what you might call the Midas touch when it came to his science, and though there was certainly a ruthlessness to his pursuit of the truth, most of the rumours about him – that he manipulated his data, that he harassed his female students, then fired them for his own mistakes – had not stood up to scrutiny. There were stories of women who had come close to him, of men too, but even if they were true the affairs can't have lasted long because I never heard the same name repeated twice. He was the object of great admiration, but also, inevitably, of envy. The head of the anatomy department explained to me, not unkindly, that my part in the sleep project mattered very little to the maestro. He was far more deeply involved in another series of experiments, the brainchild of a brilliant young student from East Germany, which involved tweaking the circadian rhythms of mice, sending them to sleep and waking them up again with the wave of a chemical wand.

Later he moved on to other questions. How much of the world do our waking brains perceive? Do we log every new detail, every change in our environment, or are we more slapdash? Do we sample it crudely and fill in the gaps from memory, from imagination? But those experiments, the ones with the sleeping mice, were the ones for which he would be remembered. They won him the prize and secured him the directorship of the new brain sciences institute. A certain type of patient came to see him as their hero and saviour. People in the street, even the healthy ones, knew his name – but only long after his work had already changed their lives in subtle ways they could never imagine.

What happened to the East German prodigy, Franz Kalb, I don't know. I never heard of him again. My insomniacs fell by the wayside, but perhaps my hard work was noticed, or perhaps (as I prefer to think) I unwittingly offered Mezzanotte some small insight that prodded him along the road to fame, because I was handsomely rewarded for my efforts. Once a year, sometimes less often, sometimes more, he would invite me back to work for him, to census and survey a certain patient population, or even just to observe and describe a single, unusual case. Even after I had left the city, the summons would find me, whichever town I happened to be working in at the time. I accepted without a second thought, working overtime so as not to annoy my boss. I could always count on the work being interesting, and even if I was kept in the dark as to where it was leading, I felt myself a part of something grand and momentous; a universal movement towards the light. Because I knew in a general sense what the adventure held for me, the day the summons arrived was always a day of great joy. I would walk around the hospital with a smile on my lips and a feeling that I had been singled out for some special purpose.

The professor and I never spoke more than was necessary, we met only to discuss the work, but I remember every detail of those meetings: how he reclined in his chair and pressed his clasped hands down on his springy brown curls when meditating on a problem; the greedy look that came into his eye when he thought he had found the solution; his habit, when the solution eluded him, of standing up suddenly, circling the desk and coming to a halt somewhere behind me. There he would linger for a few minutes, quite still and without making a sound – like one of those hawks you see hovering over the motorway verge, waiting for a small woodland creature to stray into the space beneath its talons. I don't know if he was looking at me, or if he was even aware of my presence, but the hairs on the back of my neck would stand up anyway. I came to recognise those moments as the calm before the storm, the brief interlude during which he dismantled his conscious mind and waited for some insight to well up from the depths. I would sit perfectly still, not daring to move in case I broke the spell. It was rare that an idea didn't occur to him, but on the few occasions that happened I would be summarily dismissed, without explanation or platitudes. In the early days I used to wonder why he asked me there at all, so little did I contribute. But it seems that in some strange way I was necessary to him, if only as a sounding board, a witness.

Over the years I thought I discerned a subtle change in his attitude towards me: an increase in warmth. At some point he started to call me by my first name, Sarah, but even then it didn't occur to me to call him by anything other than his proper title. Our relationship was rooted firmly in the old-fashioned, continental tradition of respect for your elders; of maintaining a formal distance between master and pupil. Only once did I venture too close. During one of our meetings I was distracted, and when he asked me where my mind was I blurted out news of a tragic event that had happened to me, the loss of someone I had loved. He merely turned to gaze out of the window, and when he spoke again, it was to continue the scientific discussion where we had left it off.

That was early on, when I was still soft in places. I didn't know what I had done to offend him, I was in turmoil for days, and he never enlightened me. I had the impression that he was a very private, if ambitious man. My admiration for him anyway verged on the unconditional, not only because he provided me with a lifeline during those dull years in the sticks, but also because I had seen him at work, and known myself to be in the presence of a great mind. Some time later, after I had taken the decision to throw myself into my work, to make that the focus of my life, things changed. Rather, my view of him changed. It came to me out of the blue one day: without knowing anything about him, I was probably the person closest to him in the world, and vice versa.

But I'm getting ahead of myself. I had been at the hospital three years, and in that time I hadn't heard a whisper from him. It was a longer silence than usual, but that didn't worry me. I felt sure, though he had never explicitly told me, that he followed my work closely through the journals, perhaps also through word of mouth. He never neglected to congratulate me on a paper that had received polite reviews, and his praise was a source of great pride to me. I ran over it in my mind for days afterwards, savouring every word. He watched my star steadily rise, and I strove not to disappoint him. I knew also that as sure as summer follows spring, I would one day receive a note from him, asking me to return to what he called my 'real' work.

At last it came. It was a cold afternoon towards the end of January, the last in a week of freezing fogs and snowstorms. The sky beyond the window was darkening, the lights across the way burned more brightly than usual. I was working on a difficult case, a lawyer from Cardiff who, following a car accident and a mild concussion, had reported seeing things: ants filing across his pillow, bears crouching in corners. He suffered from hallucinations, all right, but since his accident he had become immune to the common-or-garden visual illusions – the Necker cube, Escher's reversible staircase or some of the other ambiguous images.

My intuition told me that this was one of those rare gems that had something important to teach me, something fundamental about the nature of consciousness, and I felt the stirrings of excitement. What switch had been thrown in the lawyer's brain, that illusion had become reality and reality illusion for him? If fate hadn't intervened, it might have been that lawyer, rather than Patient DL, with whom my destiny was to become entangled. But Mezzanotte decreed otherwise. As I sat at my desk on that winter afternoon, poring over my papers, oblivious to the approaching storm, one of my assistants came into my office and handed me a note. It was unsigned, but I recognised the handwriting immediately. Without a word to my assistant, I put aside the lawyer's file and walked out of the room.

The first snowflake fell as I turned into one of the narrow tunnels that led to the outside world and, just as I emerged into the city traffic, the blizzard broke. I hurried through the swirling air, groping my way along the familiar route, until the snowstorm began to subside and I found myself standing in front of the new institute, which towered above me like a beacon against the purple sky, its giant windows ablaze. When I entered I found myself at the centre of a swarming, excited crowd. A symposium seemed to have just broken up and young men and women were flinging themselves through the sprung doors of the lecture theatre and dispersing in all directions, as if in a hurry to put what they had just learned into effect.

I stopped a young man with starry, bespectacled eyes who told me I would find the professor in his office. He had excused himself from the lecture on the grounds that he was tied up with an important experiment. I took the lift to the top floor, nodded at the two secretaries whose desks flanked his door, and knocked. Hearing no response, at a signal from the senior of the two ladies, I opened the door slightly, put my head around it and caught my breath. Across a large expanse of blue carpet, the professor was seated behind his desk, his back to a window beyond which the whole city was laid out, sparkling. The river kinked just there, beneath him, a black hole in the centre of the picture which drew to its edges the densest part of the galaxy of light. The disembodied dome of the cathedral gleamed beyond his left shoulder, and cranes loomed over the landscape like ponderous dinosaurs, lit up by Christmas lights. He was beckoning to me with a long, slender finger, then carrying it to his lips to indicate that I should not speak.

I approached his desk and stood there, waiting for him to finish. I took the opportunity to observe him. He was, by then, in his mid-sixties. His curls had turned white and fanned back from his noble forehead in a crenellated shock, lending him an air of distinction that was accentuated by the ivory cravat. Since I had seen him last, new creases had scored his forehead and lines ran down from the corners of his eyes like guy ropes. They seemed to lend his now rather gaunt face a new mobility, as if a mask had been peeled away or melted. The eyes were as dark and soulful as ever. A number of rubber pads were attached to his forehead and temples, and from these sprouted plastic-coated wires. Around him, on the desk, were arranged various grey metal boxes covered with knobs, dials and colourful, blinking lights. The professor was staring intently at a computer monitor whose greenish light threw into sharp relief the deep fissures in his face.

After a few minutes, with a sigh of expended effort, he pushed the monitor round so that I could read the words that were written there: 'Good afternoon, Sarah. I, Mezzanotte, invite you humbly, and through the medium of my slow cortical potentials, to immerse yourself once again in your work.'

It hadn't escaped my notice that there was no keyboard on the desk, and for a moment I was confused. How had he magicked the words on to the screen? He watched me, a little smile playing about his lips. And then he opened his arms as if to embrace the grey boxes scattered around him. These, he informed me, represented the culmination of three years' work. He had been following a hunch, and if it turned out to be correct, it would draw all the other threads of his scientific enquiry together; it would make sense of his life's work. He considered it the greatest idea of his career; more important than his sleep experiments, and far more audacious. He had proved it in principle (here he nodded towards the screen), and now the time had come to test it in the real world – the task for which he had summoned me.

'Here I am,' I said, my pulse quickening. 'Give me my instructions.'

At a sign from him I dragged a chair to the desk, sat down and rested my elbows on top of it. He lowered his head towards mine. And for the next hour, perhaps two, I listened in mounting awe as he explained the conception, gestation and birth of a revolutionary device – one he had developed secretly, and whose potential, he hinted, could not even be dreamed at.

3

At the top of the screen was a cartoon apple; at the bottom a pear. In between, travelling from left to right, a thread-thin waveform. It was spiky in places and somewhat irregular, but the overall motion was of a sort of languid undulation – hypnotic, potentially, if one watched it for long enough. This, the professor explained, was a readout of his slow cortical potentials, a form of brain activity about which very little was known, except that it seemed to arise spontaneously within the grey matter in the instant preceding any thought or action. Normally, one wasn't aware of it. But it was possible, with hard work, to gain control over it; to wield it as an extra limb and make it do your will.

He asked me which fruit I preferred and I told him. 'Now watch,' he said, and like a whip the wave leapt up out of its resting place and lashed the apple-shaped icon, causing it to disappear. I glanced at his hands, which had remained neatly and conspicuously folded in his lap, and laughed. I asked him how long he had been practising.

'Oh, a couple of months,' he said, his cheeks glowing with

pleasure and the mental effort of executing that trivial action. As he spoke, his large, elegant hands on which the veins stood out proud and blue acted out what he was telling me. 'To begin with, I had to conjure up certain mental images to get the wave to move the way I wanted. I remembered a circus that came one summer to my grandmother's village. I was the ringmaster, wielding my whip, and those . . .' he wagged a disapproving finger at the icons on the screen, '. . . those were a couple of bolshie lions. Or I thought about the local farmer raising his rifle, waiting for the she-wolf to move into his sights, squeezing the trigger, bullseye! It was hard work, every evening I'd go home with a headache. But slowly, slowly it got easier. Now I manipulate that wave as easily as lifting my arm, or breathing. I don't think about it. And these days, I hardly make any errors.'

In place of the fruit the letters A and B now appeared on the screen. Again I chose and this time, to show off his neural dexterity, Mezzanotte persuaded the wave to rise slowly and steadily towards the A, until it glanced off the foot of it, nudging it gently into oblivion.

'What you have here,' he went on, unnecessarily, since I had already grasped its significance, 'is a simple method of communication.' He pressed a button so that two banks of letters now appeared at the top and bottom of the screen. Each bank contained half the alphabet. 'Each time I select a bank it halves, until I'm left with the letter I want. Gradually, by this method, I can construct a word.'

He added that what I was seeing was actually an early prototype. He had a more advanced model, into which he had built sophisticated features such as a dictionary, a thesaurus and a mode for predicting the word from the first few letters typed. My mind raced ahead. 'So someone who has lost the power of speech, due to a stroke, say, or a road accident . . . motor neurone disease –'

'– someone whose output pathways are irreparably damaged,' Mezzanotte interrupted me, 'assuming of course they have something to say, could bypass the inert tongue or larynx and communicate via these brainwaves. All she would need would be the equipment. No dutiful secretary sitting by the bed, trying to make sense of her nods and grunts. Just willpower, a little mental application and a computer.'

'But Professor, it's brilliant. How did you –' I broke off, having just noticed his use of the feminine pronoun, and glanced at him. 'You already have a volunteer?'

Gripping a bunch of wires with one hand, he tore the suction pads off his forehead with a series of loud pops, stood up and strode out into that sea of carpet, where he began to stride up and down. I twisted in my chair to keep him in my sights.

'Once I'd shown the system could work, the next step was to find a subject,' he was saying. 'So I sat down to write out a list of my requirements. I discounted at a stroke all those whose insult has left them with some residual motor function, who can mumble or blink or point. That type of patient can make their basic needs understood, and rather like a Spanish speaker in Italy, it makes them lazy. They don't need to bother with my wires and waves and bolshie lions, the thought of which will quite literally make their heads ache.

No, the patient who puts the Mind-Reading Device through its paces must be completely paralysed. She must be unable to nod, to signal yes or no, food or water, pleasure or pain. She is mute, and utterly dependent on those who care for her. Nurses dress her, machines feed her. In fact, you might say she has lost all dignity. She must be a quick learner, ideally young. Above all, she must understand my instructions and appreciate the rewards her efforts will bring.'

I thought for a moment. 'Paralysed, but her intellect intact . . . a prisoner . . .'

He crossed the room rapidly towards me, resting one hand on the back of my chair and narrowing his eyes as he looked down at me. 'I don't need to tell you, Sarah, how many patients fit that bill.'

I completed the thought: 'And how few of them we ever hear about.' Mezzanotte nodded, smiled, and resumed his seat behind the desk.

I had seen some of those patients, shut away in back bedrooms or, if the families had money, in care homes in dismal seaside resorts. There were more and more of them, kept alive by modern technology. For the most part they led pathetic lives, cared for by relatives who saw them as nothing but a nuisance. Those whose families still held out hope of a cure were rare indeed. When you found one, they were usually against all experimentation. They were afraid it would be too taxing for the patient, or raise false hopes.

The professor continued. He had been searching for a suitable subject for months, in vain, when he had received a letter. The woman who wrote it said she was at her wits' end. Her daughter had been lying in hospital for a decade, without lifting a finger or uttering a word. The doctors had so far been unable to do anything for her, but she and her husband continued to hope for a cure, or at least a partial recovery. They were prepared to wait for as long as it took, but matters had been taken out of their hands when, a few months earlier, the girl's husband had announced his intention to draw the family's ordeal to a close, and end her life. This outcome the mother would resist 'with her last breath'. She had written to Mezzanotte in desperation, on the strength of his reputation alone, to beg him to find a way to help her daughter before it was too late.

The ground had been prepared for me, he went on. A technician in the department had offered his services. The doctors at the hospital had been briefed, the nursing staff was standing by. The team was assembled, all except for one member, in many ways the most important. He paused for effect. 'As I see it, you will be the hub of the wheel, and the rest of us the spokes. It will be your responsibility to oversee the patient's training, to observe her responses and adjust the schedule accordingly. You will relay her needs to us and we'll tweak the device to accommodate them. That way, it will develop in parallel with her. If everything goes according to plan, I predict that this young woman, who has not spoken for ten years, will be chattering away in a matter of months. Weeks, even.'

My heart was racing. With a pretence of nonchalance I got up and strolled towards the bookshelves that lined one wall to confront a row of thick tomes: a medical dictionary, *Gray's Anatomy*, a slimmer volume written by the professor, entitled simply, *Perchance to Dream*. A patient who had been shut off from the world for a decade and to whom we might now restore the power of speech, I said to myself with a little tremor of excitement. If we gave a voice to her, what was to stop us doing the same for hundreds, perhaps thousands of others? What insights she could offer us. What potential there was for learning about the effects of paralysis on the brain, the rearrangements in its structure and function, the compensation, recruitment of previously redundant areas, changes in sensory function, personality, consciousness . . . the possibilities were endless. And yet, it seemed already as if the opportunity were slipping through my fingers. There was too much work for me at the hospital, and my assistants were not yet experienced enough to deal with the harder cases. I would never get permission to manage an intensive training routine such as this patient would undoubtedly need, especially if she was far away. At best, I envisaged a long return trip each day; at worst, I would have to find accommodation close to her, and that would mean requesting several months' leave. But I hadn't been in my post long enough to have earned a sabbatical. Was I really to be offered the most interesting case of my career to date, just as my duties became so onerous as to rule it out?

I heard a drawer open and close, and looked back at the professor, whose hands were now resting on a piece of paper. I sauntered back towards him. Playing for time, I asked him again who the patient was. DL, he called her, using the convention in the medical literature of referring to patients in single case studies by their initials alone. And having delivered this tiny morsel of information, as if it should be enough to satisfy me, he settled back in his chair, pressed his fingertips together and brought his quizzical gaze to rest on me.

I lowered my eyes. It had never occurred to me that I would have to choose between the professor and the job I had always dreamed of. I felt torn between my loyalty to him, my desire to help him and to be a party to the glorious climax of his career, and my love of the job he had, to a certain extent, groomed me for.

'Is she far away?' I asked, quietly.

I heard him pick up the paper he had been guarding from my sight, and push it across the desk towards me. I raised my eyes and saw that it was a typed, formal letter of consent. From the two short paragraphs of text printed there, the name of our hospital leapt out at me. I blinked at it, barely understanding what it meant.

'She's been under your nose all this time,' he said, and laughed.

4

It was dark when I stepped out into the street, but this time with nightfall. It must only recently have stopped snowing, though, because the snow had settled in an even layer over the pavement and was almost undisturbed by footprints. The night was cold, and a three-quarter moon shone crisply over the city. The people in the streets were uniformly muffled in coats and scarves.

I made my way back to the hospital, deep in thought over the professor's new project, and it was only when I stood in the large entrance hall that I became fully aware of my surroundings. It was deserted just then, though echoing footsteps receded down one of the long corridors. And it was dark; it occurred to me that a couple of light bulbs must have blown. The globe lamps on the walls had been switched on, but they seemed to shine rather weakly and hardly to penetrate the polished black slate floor. The gloom deepened towards the centre of the space, where the signpost stood. But the signpost itself was bathed in the moonlight whose shafts entered via glass panels in the ceiling. All in all, it was a ghostly scene.

The clock above the corridor that led to the north wing showed six o'clock. I had intended to go straight up to the fifth floor and introduce myself, if that's the right expression, to Patient DL. I hesitated. They would soon be serving supper on the wards. DL wouldn't be eating, of course, since she received her nutrients through a tube that fed through her nose, down her oesophagus and into her stomach. But there would be activity on the ward, and perhaps the general commotion would distract someone with a potentially tenuous grip on reality. Better to go in the morning, I decided, when it was quiet and she had a good night's sleep behind her. After ten years, one more night wouldn't make any difference.

At that moment, a figure stepped out from behind the signpost and moved in a wide semicircle towards me. It seemed to walk on the balls of its feet, in a strange sort of dance, and I recognised Nestor. He often loitered around the entrance hall. He was employed by the university as a technician, though most people still thought of him as a porter, because that had been his job for many years. He had the porter's inside knowledge of the hospital, and more. He knew every cracked pipe, every broken window latch, as well as which nurses were sleeping together and who among the registrars had played angel of death on the wards. People who worked there were afraid of him. Everyone knew that he liked his drink. But sometimes he disappeared for days at a time, and although people whispered about his absences, and his rumoured forays on to the upper floors at night, nobody dared question him openly.

The latest rumour was that he had been barred from the paediatric wing. I had no idea if it was true, but here was Nestor in front of me, rocking back and forth on the balls of his feet, asking if I would like to accompany him down to his room. 'Why would I want to do that?' I asked, amused. He raised a hand to touch the rolled-up cigarette that was tucked behind his ear, smirked and said he was surprised Mezzanotte hadn't explained. He had agreed to operate the Mind-Reading Device. The latest version of it was downstairs in his room, and he was under instructions to show it to me at my earliest convenience.

'You?' I asked, surprised. Puffing out his chest, he tapped it with a tar-stained forefinger. Perhaps I was still looking at him sceptically, because he glanced quickly over his shoulder, then brought his round, slightly greasy face close to mine and muttered that all the other technicians had refused. He wore his grey, wispy hair long on his neck. He was dressed neatly in grey flannels and a brown pullover, with a knitted green tie. It was hard to put an age on him, somewhere between forty and sixty, but there was something of the overgrown schoolboy about him. He wore a gold stud in his left ear, and around his right eye there were traces of a bruise. 'Let's go,' I said.

He danced off with the same bizarre gait, his bony rump high in the air, as if he were walking on hot coals. I followed him through an unmarked door that opened off the entrance hall, just to the right of the corridor that led to the north wing. We descended a flight of concrete steps and passed along a corridor lit by a single neon tube.

It was the first time I had been down to the basement. Stacked up on the floor along both sides of the corridor were hundreds of derelict computers, models five or six years old, some covered in old sheets, others in a thick layer of dust. Their keyboards had been thrown down haphazardly between them, and fraying wires stuck out in places. Some of the screens were shattered, as if someone had deliberately put a boot through them. Nestor mumbled something about skeletons. When I asked him what he had said, he stopped, turned to face the phalanx of defunct hardware, and announced that I was walking through the graveyard of a computer system that had once been installed in the hospital.

The idea, apparently, had been to transfer all the patients' records on to an electronic database. Ours was to be the first paperless hospital in the country, and if it worked, others would follow. But the computer hard disks turned out to have a flaw in them. Records were irretrievably lost, referrals sent to the wrong department. There were actually empty beds in the hospital for the first time, a fact that was trumpeted in the newspapers until it became clear that the sick were still waiting to fill them, their names had merely been wiped from the computer's memory. There were stories of patients dying of treatable tumours that had been diagnosed twelve months earlier, because their notes had gone astray.

I listened to all this in amazement. I wanted to know why the scandal hadn't come to light. Nestor snickered. There were many things he could tell me about this hospital, he said.

Nothing was quite as it seemed. For instance, had I heard about the geriatric ward that had been closed off due to a superbug infection? Ten beds decommissioned because two of the 'inmates', as he called them, had died. One of them only after he had been discharged and welcomed back into the bosom of his family. The rest of the occupants had been put into quarantine, since the infection, once contracted, did not respond to antibiotics. Naturally the administration wanted to avoid a panic. Nestor had seen for himself the locked door and discreet notice barring entrance to the ward. He could show me if I liked. I told him that wouldn't be necessary, and he turned down the corners of his mouth, as if to say, 'Please yourself.'

We came to a door marked 'W.E. Nestor. No Unauthorised Entry.' He pulled a key from his pocket and unlocked it, switching on the light inside. More electronic and mechanical equipment was stacked around the walls of the small, windowless room, and directly ahead of me, as I stood in the doorway, was a wooden chair in front of a folding card table. Above the card table, which was covered in green baize, torn in places, a small wooden cross was tacked to the wall. Grey boxes identical to the ones I had seen in Mezzanotte's office were arranged on the table around a computer monitor, and hanging over one corner of the chair was a sort of outsized, rose-coloured swimming cap with a tail of wires sprouting from it. A sinister-looking object, like some instrument of psychic torture.

Nestor was telling me that he had adapted and improved the device; put some 'finishing touches' to it. The electrodes were now woven into this soft, plastic helmet so that you no longer had to attach the pads one by one. He nodded in the direction of the table, indicating that I should sit down, and I did so. Then he picked up the helmet and without further ado, levered it first over the plates at the top of my skull, then the jutting bones at the base of it, sending a shudder down my spine. I gritted my teeth as he adjusted the cap on the forehead and tucked the hair deftly beneath it at the nape. Gathering the tail of wires he swept it over my shoulder so that it lay heavily against my back and didn't impede my movements. Then he stepped back, folded his arms over his chest and said, 'There!'

'Can we get on with it?' I said, crossly, and with an injured look he leaned forward to switch on the computer monitor. As the screen resolved itself, I saw that the layout was still the same. At the top was an apple, at the bottom a pear. Equidistant between the two undulated a horizontal line. He switched off the lights and melted into the darkness behind me. Closing my eyes I conjured up a ringmaster, faceless, resplendent in red, the polish high on his leather belt and boots. Idly twirling the whip at his hip, so that it stirred up flurries of sawdust, he waited for the lions to settle. Against my closed eyelids, one of the beasts yawned and looked round, as if preparing to climb down off its box. The ringmaster raised his whip arm high above his head and, 'Yah!', cracked it in the air . . . The lion stared at him, frozen in flesh and time. I opened my eyes. The line flowed on, unperturbed. I repeated the exercise three or four times and the same thing happened each time, until in exasperation I turned to Nestor.

'It doesn't work.'

He had been sitting quietly at the side of the room. I could just see him, his chair tipped back against the wall, lovingly fingering his rolled-up cigarette. Now he stuck it back behind his ear and brought his chair down with a clack. I had to remember that the machine had not been designed with me in mind, he said. It was supposed to be used by someone who was desperate to communicate, and for whom it provided the only means of doing so.

'You mean I'm not trying hard enough?'

He shrugged. That was part of it, he said, and then there were the lions. 'They don't do it for me.'

I asked him how he had made it work, but he didn't want to say. I cajoled him a bit and he hung his head coyly. I pleaded with him until at last, with some excited shifting in his seat, he came out with it. 'I'm riding an old Enfield through a deserted city. I come to a red light where another bike is waiting. The rider revs his engine, he glances across at me. I recognise the head porter. Well, between you and me, I hate the head porter. I turn back to the lights, I watch them like a hawk. Red changes to red and amber, I tighten my grip. Green! I release the clutch, leap the junction and land on two wheels, leaving him trailing in the dust . . .'

He had been talking eagerly from the edge of his seat. But now he slid back into the shadows and I turned once again to face the computer monitor. It seemed to me that he had hit on a good device. There was a certain elastic tension in that sequence: red, red and amber, green. I frowned hard at the undulating line. But however hard I concentrated, I couldn't interrupt it. Finally, I let out the breath I had been holding.

'It's no good,' I said, 'it won't budge.'

For a moment there was silence, and then out of the darkness behind me came a voice.

'It's got to mean something to you,' it said softly. 'You've really got to want it.'

I sat staring disconsolately at the screen, raising a finger at one point to scratch an itch at my temple, just under the rim of the cap. But I had no ideas. And then I did have an idea. It came to me out of the blue. Thankfully it was dark in the room and my face was turned away from Nestor, so he couldn't see how I blushed. Once again I pictured the ringmaster, dashing in jodhpurs and a red tunic pulled in at the waist by a thick leather belt. This time, however, he wore an ivory cravat and a shock of white hair rose from his high forehead. Taking a step towards the lions he planted the soles of his riding boots wide apart in the sawdust, cracked his whip and fixed them with his burning, soulful gaze. I stared at the undulating line and to my amazement it lurched drunkenly towards the pear, missing it by a hair's breadth.

Suddenly the room was a blaze of electric light, and I spun round in time to see Nestor bring his hand down from the wall switch. His body was rigid in the chair against the wall. He was staring sulkily at his cigarette and a muscle was flickering in his cheek. What's the matter with him? I thought. Is he annoyed that someone else besides him has made his precious machine work? I peeled off the pink swimming cap, draped it over a corner of the chair and stood up. Nestor remained sitting, his head bowed. Just as I reached the door, a thought struck me.

'Have you seen the patient?' I asked. He raised his head slowly and I noticed that the eye around which there were traces of bruising was also bloodshot.

'Should I have?'

There was menace in his voice, and I was taken aback. I told him it was an innocent question. He slammed the two front legs of his chair against the floor, standing up as he did so and clenching his fists. He had no reason to go snooping around up on the fifth floor, he said, and he'd like to know who'd seen him there. Furiously he kicked at a screwed-up ball of paper, sending it flying into the corner. Then he seemed to calm down again, and scuffed the toe of his boot sheepishly against the floor. I asked him why the other technicians had refused to work with the professor. He shrugged. I pressed him and he told me that Mezzanotte was in the habit of ringing up at midnight to discuss a problem. Sometimes he wanted the technician to meet him straight away, at the lab, and the poor fellow might not get away before dawn. It was hard on a man. But it was no skin off his nose.

I raised an eyebrow. 'You don't need to sleep?'

He frowned, irritated. He needed to sleep as much as the next man, but he had to take pills to bring it on, and these days the pills didn't seem to work as well as they used to. So he was often awake in the early hours. He didn't approve of the professor's working habits, but as it happened they suited him. He was the man for the job, and Mezzanotte would have saved a lot of time if he had come straight to him, rather than letting his mind be poisoned by 'filthy lies'.

I looked at him. So he was an insomniac. That explained a few things, and yet it didn't arouse any sympathy in me. 'Good evening, Mr Nestor,' I said, and stepped out into the corridor.

Back in my rooms everything was in order. My assistants had left for the night, and a note on my desk assured me that the afternoon had passed off well, and nothing out of the ordinary had happened. Two or three files had been placed over that of the Welsh lawyer's: new cases awaiting my attention. I hesitated, wondering whether to sit down and make a start on them. Just then a wave of fatigue came over me and I raised my eyes to the window.

My own face was reflected against the night: a pale moon with two dark ovals for eyes, framed by short, thick, reddish-gold hair. Beyond my reflection, or rather through it, were the lighted windows of the operating theatres. I knew that at this hour it could only be the cleaners at work up there, but the sight still had a soothing effect on me, for the reasons I've explained. Then suddenly it didn't. The hospital seemed to crowd in on the axis of our two sets of windows, upsetting that precious symmetry. Three floors above me, Patient DL lay on her back as she had done for a decade, beyond the reach of medicine. Down in the basement, hundreds of obsolete hard disks harboured the records of patients who would never recover. In their midst, Nestor tinkered with his new toy, awaiting the hour when, if the rumour was true, he would set off on his nightly tour of the hospital. He would throw the switch on his way out, so that the only source of light in the room would be the greenish glow of the computer screen: that snakelike waveform I had managed at last to displace – though not, perhaps, in the way Mezzanotte had intended. Hurriedly I turned my back on my own reflection, crossed the room and locked the door behind me.

5

The next morning I returned to the hospital. As the lift rose past the second floor, then the third, I prepared myself mentally for the meeting to come. I had never yet dealt with a patient whose injuries were so severe, or whose diagnosis was as uncertain as that of Patient DL's. I told myself that she was no different from the rest, only a little further along the spectrum, the scale of handicap, and that therefore I should treat her no differently. Even if she appeared not to respond to my attempts to communicate with her, I should continue to address her in the belief that she understood. I repeated the mantra over and over in my head: she's no different, she's no different. But I couldn't quite drown out the small voice that said, there is something quite unusual about this patient and you know it. The upshot of this internal wrangling was that I was nervous, and several times as the lift rose, wiped the sweaty palms of my hands on the seat of my trousers.

When the doors opened at the fifth floor the first thing that struck me was the silence. It was thick, almost palpable, and when I glanced towards a window, and saw beyond it an overcast sky punctured by a few high-rise buildings, I realised with a shock that I had never set foot on this floor before. I had dealt with patients in hospitals on the other side of the world, but this was the first time I had ventured on to the fifth floor of my own. The fourth floor was where I had conducted most of my business, where the patients were, generally speaking, responsive. The silence was like a challenge to me: is there really anything you can do here? it seemed to say. Aren't you out of your depth?

I presented myself at the charge nurse's desk. She gave me a friendly smile and when she spoke her voice seemed to ring out too loudly, though in fact, I realised afterwards, she spoke at a normal volume. She checked her list and informed me that the patient had no visitors at the moment. It was still only eight thirty. Her first visitor of the day would arrive at nine. 'And who will that be?' I asked.

'Her father,' she replied. 'He comes every morning and sits with her for an hour. A nice old gentleman. Quiet as a mouse.'

She pointed towards the mouth of a long corridor whose walls had been painted dark green up to waist height and cream above, with a long, narrow, black line separating the two. These were the colours that indicated the public areas of the hospital, though public and private lost their significance on this ward, where the patients were so ill they required round-the-clock care to keep them alive. In keeping with the hospital code, though, there was also blue linoleum underfoot, rather than carpet. The only thing that set this ostensibly public ward apart from the real public wards lower down was that each patient had his or her own room – on lower floors, and along with carpet, the exclusive privilege of private patients who paid for their care.

The corridor stretched off into the further reaches of the wing. I followed it and turned right where it formed a ninety-degree angle, and left where it formed a second. As I moved further away from the nurse's station and, as it seemed to me, the living heart of the ward, the silence grew thicker still. I've never been to a morgue, but I suspect that if I had it would sound something like that. The notices occasionally taped up by the doors might not be worded so differently either. One read: 'Do not enter without gloves or apron', another: 'Latex allergy'. Slowly my ear grew attuned, and I began to detect the sounds of frail, struggling life: the hum and occasional click of life-support machinery. The rhythmic expansion and contraction of twenty diaphragms. The faint, almost inaudible breathing of creatures trapped between life and death.

I found myself making efforts to walk soundlessly, not to let my shoes squeak on the linoleum. Eventually I came to the last room on the corridor. It had no notice pinned up outside it, but the door was open and glancing inside I was struck by the sight of a shiny balloon floating in a yellow haze. A child's birthday balloon, filled with helium. Semi-deflated now, with the words 'Happy Birthday!' looping across it, it bobbed at half mast and a low voice seemed to emanate from it. As I stepped over the threshold, I realised that the voice actually came from a TV suspended on the wall above and behind me. I naturally turned to look at the woman lying in the bed, whose line of vision I had broken, and that's when I got the fright of my life. Her brown eyes were fixed on me, and in them was a steady gleam of contempt, as if the liquid of her iris had crystallised that way. I froze, and in the instant that our eyes met I half expected her to rear up and point an imperious finger out into the corridor. But her gaze merely slid away from me and became liquid again.

Feeling like a clumsy intruder, my heart hammering against my ribs, I lifted the clipboard out of its slot at the foot of the bed and pretended to peruse the drug chart. My hands were trembling, but I forced myself to focus on the words printed before my eyes. Name: Diane Levy. Date of birth: so-and-so. I peeped over the board. Her head lay in the same place on the pillow, but her gaze was vacant now, and dull. A thread of saliva ran from the corner of her mouth, down over her slack jaw. Breathing a sigh of relief, I glanced quickly around the room.

My first impression had been of entering a shrine or grotto, and now I saw that I wasn't far wrong. A ledge running at waist height down the side of the room facing the bed was crowded with small objects, ornaments and such like, while the wall above it was densely covered with fragments of drawings, letters and photographs. There were several vases arranged about the room, containing flowers at various stages of freshness. At the windows hung not the usual, pale, waxy hospital curtains, but ones with a flower pattern, white on blue, good cotton and properly lined. They were cheery, the sort you might find in a nursery, and obviously home-made. At the side of the bed nearest the window a rocking chair was covered with a pink, mohair rug that carried the impression of a large person's shoulders and haunches. On the other side, nearest the door, stood a plain, straight-backed wooden chair that had been pulled up close to the bed, and on this I now sat down.

From her date of birth I calculated that Diane had recently passed her thirty-first birthday. Close up, she looked younger than that. Almost childlike, as if the injury to her brain had also knocked her body's internal clock, causing it to stop. There were no blemishes on her sallow skin, not a single worry line or crease of laughter. Nothing had troubled that flawless complexion for a decade, except perhaps very fleetingly, and then only a surge in electrical activity, a bubbling over of the animal parts of her nervous system. Her hair, which had been cropped high on her neck, was tousled and shiny as a conker against the snowy-white pillowcase.

I introduced myself and explained why I was there. 'Soon some men will bring a machine,' I said, taking care to enunciate clearly. 'It will arrive in parts. I'll put them together and then I'll show you how to use it. Before you know it, you'll be able to ask for anything you want.'

Somebody was walking in the corridor outside, I heard their footfall and turned quickly. But there was no one there, and when I turned back my heart skipped a beat. Slowly, almost as slowly as Mezzanotte's brainwave had risen to graze the foot of the letter A, Diane was arching her eyebrows. They fell at the same controlled rate, and her lips stretched horizontally beneath the feeding tube inserted into her nostril. At that moment a light came into her eyes, as if someone had shone a torch through the back of her skull, and her face lit up with a joyous smile. Her lips parted and I saw her small, wet tongue lolling inside. I sucked in my breath. At that moment, as if she had achieved the desired effect, the light went out, and once again her dull gaze slid past me.

It's a reflex, I told myself, a simple reflex. But what if it wasn't? On an impulse, I leaned forward and squeezed her bony fist where it lay, immobile on the sheet, to let her know I had seen. It was cool, a little rough to the touch. I saw myself do it; from a point on the ceiling I observed my own rather secretive gesture, and I immediately felt foolish. As I straightened up and let go of her hand, I caught a whiff of something. Not the usual smell of the chronically ill, but something sugary, cloyingly sweet. A wave of nausea rose to my stomach, so powerful it pushed me up to my feet and away from the bed. Mumbling something about another appointment, promising to return soon, I backed out of the room and sped away along the corridor.

6

What was that smell? At the first turn in the corridor I slowed to a walk and racked my brains to identify it. It was almost as if she were preserved in something, infused with a very weak syrup: a living cadaver. I shuddered and walked faster. Ahead of me I heard murmuring voices, two women, one of them I recognised as belonging to the charge nurse, the other deeper, more mellifluous. I emerged from the corridor, and the two women standing by the nurse's desk turned to look at me: Sister and Fleur Bartholomew, a neurologist I had worked with in the past and knew well.

'Well,' Fleur said, 'did she turn a nice somersault for you?' The nurse laughed, a mocking laugh, and when I looked at her she lowered her eyes to her chart. Fleur was regarding me steadily, but in a good-humoured way. She wore an emerald-green tunic and a towering green turban. Heavy ropes of amber beads hung around her neck, and her teeth when she smiled were like a slash of white in her polished, black face.

'She smiled at me,' I said. 'I mean, I know it wasn't . . . but it really seemed as if she smiled.'

I felt the blood rush to my cheeks. Fleur laughed, a deep booming laugh like a train rumbling underground, and opened her eyes to show the yellowish whites. 'Voodoo, is it?'

I glanced at the nurse, who was smirking under her blonde eyelashes, and I asked Fleur if I could talk to her privately.

We took the lift to the third floor. The hospital lifts were old and slow, we descended with rattles and jolts. I leaned in the corner and chewed my lip, watching Fleur as she adjusted her turban in front of the mirror that covered the back wall, but without, so to speak, really seeing her. My mind was still occupied with my recent encounter. I was surprised and annoyed at myself for having been put so easily off my stride. It was as if no time had passed since my immersion in the strange world of insomnia, as if I had learned nothing from that episode and all the patients who had passed through my consulting room since. This patient had plucked emotions from me as effortlessly as if she were picking daisies, and the nurse and Fleur had seen it written on my face.

The lift stopped at the fourth floor but the doors didn't open. It remained stationary for a minute or two, as if confused. Fleur hummed a bit, and rustled inside her silk sheath as she swung her hips out to left and right. Then, as if she had been reading my mind, she threw me a sidelong glance and told me not to tie myself up in knots. As soon as she said it, I realised how tensely I had been holding myself. Her drawing attention to it seemed to release something inside me, and in the small, enclosed space of the lift, where nobody could hear us, I told her everything I had seen; my chaotic impressions of that first meeting. I explained that the two looks Diane had given me, the one of contempt and the other of joy, had seemed somehow *directed* at me. I had reminded myself that her facial expressions were nothing but muscular tics, I wasn't as easily led as all that, nevertheless it was uncanny. Even though I had only been in the room a few minutes, I had felt very strongly the presence of another intelligence.

Fleur waited until I had finished, then smiled. It was natural to feel that way the first time one met Diane, she said, because as a human being one identified with the most meagre spark of humanity in another living creature. I mustn't underestimate the power of wishful thinking, of *willing* her to understand. Even as a professional, it was hard not to be led astray, down the path of hope. As a professional, though, one also had to remember that there was a simpler explanation. There was almost always a simpler explanation. 'I know, I know,' I said, and slumped in the corner.

With a jolt the lift started to descend again. Fleur laughed and shook her head. Everyone went through the same storm of emotions the first time they met Diane, she said. After that, you had to come to terms with her in your own way. The way she had come to think of it was that looking at Diane was a bit like 'looking at the sea'. Everybody had their own idea about what was lurking in the depths, but they all saw the same thing: clouds reflected in the surface. I thought about this. It was a nice idea, but it wasn't enough. I wanted to say so, but Fleur had already turned back to the mirror, and raising a hand to the back of her magnificent turban, was twisting this way and that, smiling at her reflection. A moment later, the doors opened on the third floor.

A long corridor opened up before us, and I remembered that her office was at the end of it. That meant we had to walk past the operating suites on our right. One of the doors to these suites stood ajar, and when I looked through it I saw that the room was bare. All the equipment had been stripped out, including the operating table. There was just a solitary roll of bandage on the floor, partially unravelled. I stopped and stared at it. Fleur explained that the theatres were closed for repairs. All surgery had been moved to the paediatric wing on a temporary basis. Hadn't I read the memo? No, I murmured in dismay. Somehow memos passed me by; I never found time to read them. We walked on and entered her office, which was similar to mine, except that where I had hung my framed certificates, she had photographs. In all of the pictures two children were laughing, a boy and a girl, and their smiles were identical to hers. I remarked how happy they looked and she smiled a proud, maternal smile.

We sat down in two stiff-backed armchairs covered in tartan plaid. Fleur crossed her legs and clasped her hands on her knee. Her red-lacquered nails stuck out in all directions, like the blades of a Swiss army knife. The conversation in the lift was forgotten. Now I could see from her erect posture, the way she held her head and the flash in her intelligent eyes, that she had assumed her professional hat. She explained in a matter-of-fact way that Diane's smile was nothing more than a reflex triggered by stimulation of the retina: a shape flitting across the light-sensitive surface at the back of the eye. It might be that the shape had to be human, but no one could be sure about that. 'A dog might get the same warm welcome,' she said, and laughter welled up from deep in her thorax.

'Yes, of course,' I said, ashamed, and I asked her about the sickly smell. But that was easily explained too, she said. Diane's mother assiduously massaged her with creams and lotions, to keep her skin from drying out and cracking. She was the best-oiled patient in the place; a glistening advertisement for royal jelly.

I laughed and settled back in my chair. I was feeling better now. I even said, 'I don't know what came over me,' but Fleur waved her hand languidly in the air as if to say, 'Don't give it another thought.' Then she continued to regard me with her smiling, questioning face, as if she were waiting to find out why I had come. Eventually I reminded her of what she must already know: that I was going to be working with the patient and Mezzanotte's machine, so I needed to know everything there was to know about her; every detail of her medical history. At that, she arched a pencilled eyebrow. 'He's serious, then?'

I asked her why she should doubt it, and she looked at me thoughtfully. It was two months since the professor had paid her a visit, she said, and described how he proposed to help her patient. He had asked her opinion, and she had given it: the diagnosis was uncertain, the family was split. There were certainly more suitable candidates out there. But she agreed it was an interesting case, and that if she hadn't been so busy herself, she would have liked to spend more time getting to the bottom of it. So she wouldn't stand in his way.

Since then she had assumed that he had abandoned his

plans, having come to the conclusion himself, perhaps, that they were too ambitious. The odds against it working, in the case of this particular patient, were high. I laughed. No, no, I assured her, the professor doesn't give up so easily. The project was going full steam ahead, and I was to play a central role in it. I was to oversee the patient's training.

She looked at me for a long time, with a strange expression, then raised her eyes to the ceiling. 'Let me see . . .' she mused, tugging meditatively at her long earlobe, from which a heavy gold ring dangled. 'The case came to me six years ago, when Dr Seaforth, the previous consultant, retired.'

The history was as follows. Diane Levy collapsed the day after her twenty-first birthday, on the top floor of the maisonette that she shared with her husband, Adrian. She had married the young man a year earlier, having known him for only a few months. He worked for a newspaper; she kept house and dabbled in a little painting. Until her marriage Diane had always lived with her parents. She had suffered from diabetes since early childhood and her mother had, to some extent, wrapped her in cotton wool. True, she was prone to mild vascular problems, poor circulation, and once there was a scare over her eyesight, but it turned out to be a false alarm. In fact, the chances were that she had twenty-twenty vision. It was the brain behind the eyes whose state of health, or decay, was less certain.

Soon after the Levys returned from their honeymoon in Florence, Adrian turned the top floor of their apartment into a studio for his wife. It was here that one afternoon, surrounded by her tubes of paint and brushes, her life took its sudden, tragic turn. To begin with, there was a suspicion of foul play. But the police found no evidence of a break-in and quickly ruled out the possibility that she had opened the door to her attacker. There was bruising on her neck and on the back of her head, which could have been caused by a blow, a fall, some internal, physiological process or a combination of all three. The police eventually called off their investigation. Most likely there was no third party involved, and she had merely suffered a thrombosis or clot related to her underlying diabetes. While she stood at her easel, dabbing at a canvas, it travelled through her blood vessels to the stem of her brain, where it became lodged, blocking the supply of oxygen to the cerebral organ higher up. She fell to the floor, unconscious, and was found there three hours later by her husband.

At that point Levy called an ambulance and Diane was rushed to the nearest hospital, where she remained in a coma for several days. Then she woke up. That is to say, she opened her eyes and scalp recordings of her brain's electrical activity indicated that she had recovered some form of sleep/wake cycle. It wasn't obvious from looking at her, and in all other respects her condition stayed the same. After a couple of weeks, once it had stabilised, she was flown by helicopter to this hospital where she had remained ever since.

Extending a smooth, bare arm from her voluminous green sleeve, Fleur now slid a thick dossier off the desk and, leaning forward, laid it in my lap. Lifting the cover with one finger, I took in the mass of poorly shuffled papers interleaved with glossy, grainy, black-and-white brain scans, and felt the familiar pulse of adrenalin at the prospect of a new case, a new challenge, and many different strands of evidence to marshal and make sense of. I let the cover drop, laid a protective hand over the top of it and paid attention once again to Fleur.

From the beginning, she was saying, many doctors came to examine Diane. They filed past her bed 'like cardinals at a pope's funeral'. There were certain fundamentals they all agreed on. For instance, that she could breathe by herself, but not swallow; that she had no control over her muscles, except possibly for those that allowed her to blink, and others that controlled the direction of her gaze. For all practical purposes, she was paralysed. Some of the doctors had been inclined to write her off as a hopeless case even then, but scans of her brain brought them up short. Apart from a few isolated spots of nerve cell loss, the scans showed that most of her grey matter had been preserved. The grey matter is the seat of language, thought and memory. So the puzzle then was, if she was awake and listening, if she remembered who she was and recognised the people who came into her room, why didn't she make use of her eyes to signal to them?

She hadn't. Not a sign in ten years. Only that disconcerting, mechanical smile and one or two other idiosyncratic facial tics. Over this incontrovertible fact the experts had fallen out. They simply could not agree on how much of Diane's intellect and personality remained. Having failed to reach a consensus, they had split themselves into two camps. One camp considered her to have a primitive form of consciousness; that, at best, she could recognise a familiar voice and respond to it. Beyond that, they felt, her intellectual capacities were nil. This group believed that the scans that were carried out ten years ago, when Diane first came to the hospital, were not fine enough to reveal the critical lesion, the one that had erased her mind, her soul or whatever you liked to call it. Since then science had advanced in leaps and bounds, the technology had become far more sophisticated and some of them had petitioned to have her rescanned, believing that now they would certainly find that spot of dead tissue; the physical location of her extinguished life force. But her husband had steadfastly refused, arguing that it wouldn't cure her, but it would cause her unnecessary distress. So the question remained unresolved, much to those doctors' chagrin.

The second group, by contrast, believed that there was no critical lesion. In their opinion, Diane was neurologically intact, conscious and aware of all that was going on around her, but had her own reasons for not communicating her status to the world. She was depressed, they suggested, and had retreated into herself. Perhaps, just prior to her injury, something had so shocked her that she had voluntarily turned mute. Her physical paralysis masked an emotional one. It must have been a very great shock to have silenced her for a decade. But since no psychiatrist could interview her, there was no drawing it out of her.

Fleur fell silent and turned her big brown eyes on me, as if calmly anticipating my next question.

'So,' I said, after a moment's reflection, 'to go back to your cloud metaphor, either the clouds hide shoals of fish, coral, a shipwreck or two, that is, life as we know it goes on beneath the ocean wave. Or behind the clouds there are more clouds, and more clouds behind that.'

She nodded, evidently pleased that I had been listening, and I asked her which camp she belonged to. She sighed and rolled her eyes. First, she said, she had allied herself with the optimists, those who claimed that Diane was 'in there', and all that was needed was the right incentive to lure her out. But with time, and no new evidence, she had shifted her ground. She had moved towards the pessimists, those who believed there was no hope, and that Diane's consciousness was too fragmentary to afford her any meaningful interaction with the world; that she might indeed be better off dead. I looked at the floor, momentarily gripped by the futility of the exercise. Above my head, Fleur was still speaking. 'But that didn't feel right either . . .'

I raised my eyes cautiously. She laughed, holding up the pale palms of her hands as if in surrender. '. . . so now I've set up a third camp. I call it wait-and-see camp . . .' I slipped back into the recesses of my chair and gazed at her. Then I asked her one or two more questions. There were some technical details I wanted to clarify. After that Fleur walked me to the door, her fleshy hand resting affectionately on my shoulder. She asked me to come and see her again in a fortnight. I thanked her and said I would certainly keep her abreast of developments. But she tightened her grip on my shoulder and made me promise to return, in person, in two weeks' time. By then I would have established a rapport with the patient, she said (even if that rapport existed only in my own mind), I would have met the family. Despite all my best intentions I would have been drawn into the case. She would like to make sure I didn't lose sight of the facts; to act as my anchor in the real world.

'You think she's harmless because she doesn't speak,' she added. 'But they're the most dangerous kind.'

And bending stiffly at the waist, rustling inside her silk sheath, she hugged me to her breast.

I wandered slowly back along the corridor towards the lifts, clutching the bulging dossier, mulling over all Fleur had told me and smiling at her last piece of advice. Glancing absent-mindedly into an empty room, I saw again that partially unravelled roll of bandage on the floor – the only evidence that the room had once functioned as an operating theatre – and felt the same stab of surprise as I had the first time I saw it, just half an hour earlier. I gazed at it for a moment, then walked on to where the lift doors stood open and waiting for me.

7

Back in my office I set Patient DL's notes aside and turned my attention to the files already there. Opening one I settled down to read it, but I kept seeing that partially unravelled roll of bandage in my mind's eye. I glanced over my shoulder at the lights on the third floor opposite, knowing now that those rooms were empty and the light came from the corridor beyond. It didn't help to tell myself that the operations were going on as usual, in another part of the hospital, because the fact was that they were no longer there, where they should have been. Knowing that ruined my concentration.

I gave up trying to read, got up from my desk and walked out of my office. Seeing one of my assistants helping a young man on a crutch limp into his room, I told him I had been called to see a patient in the geriatric wing and that I would be back as soon as possible.

The entrance hall was busy. Porters were crossing it in different directions, briskly pushing patients in wheelchairs. A family stood near the signpost looking lost and a female guide was giving a tour to a group of men in suits, who with their heads tipped back, were politely inspecting the stained-glass window above the great door, which depicted various ancient and obsolete forms of healing. I walked past them, heading in the direction of the geriatric wing.

As I've explained, the paediatric and geriatric wings were smaller than the north wing and had no gardens of their own. However, the geriatric wing did have one distinguishing feature: a small, circular chapel built just beyond the end of it, which was reached by a gravel path that extended from a door in the wall of the building. This chapel was of a rather unusual design. Inside, it was arranged on a hexagonal plan, with six recesses facing a central pulpit. In the days when the hospital was an asylum, each alcove would accommodate a different category of patient, who were prevented from seeing the others but had a full view of the priest at the centre. At the time, the prevailing wisdom was that the different varieties of insanity mixed badly, so it was thought that the drunks should be separated from the suicides who should not be allowed to mingle with the prostitutes.

This chapel was where I now headed. There was no one else there, and I sat down in one of the empty recesses, breathing in the odour of warm stone and wood polish. I am not religious, but I believe that churches are the last corners of our cities that are conducive to quiet reflection. Perhaps because no one goes there any more. And for that very reason, perversely, people might come back to God.

A chapel in the geriatric wing of a hospital is quieter than most, and this was where I went when I wanted to think through a knotty problem. After a few minutes I heard the heavy door of the chapel open and then the slow shuffling of feet and the rhythmic tap of a cane. It sounded, from their muffled voices, like two old men. They sat down in the recess next to mine, close to the wall against which I leaned, and continued their conversation in hushed tones. Their quavering, feeble voices, issuing no doubt through false teeth, rose up to the vaulted ceiling and echoed round the walls. I let the soft, insipid sound wash over me, but at one point one of them said something that made me prick up my ears.

'Latimer is off-limits,' he said, and I recognised the name of one of the geriatric wards. I didn't catch the other's reply, something about a sore throat. Then the first said that was how it started, with a ticklish throat. He for one didn't intend to hang about, he had a good mind to discharge himself that afternoon, even though he didn't know how he'd manage by himself, especially when it came to his dressings. I waited to hear what else they would say. But the conversation turned into a dispute over a card game and I lost interest. The volume of the old men's voices gradually increased until it became intrusive, and I was obliged to clear my throat. They broke off their argument in a surprised silence. A few minutes later I heard the tap of a stick and more shuffling, and then the heavy oak door open and close.

My thoughts turned to Mezzanotte. As the daughter of immigrants myself (my surname, Newman, is adopted, my real one being harder to pronounce), I took in with my mother's milk the idea that my rightful place was a little apart from the centre of things; that I should keep a respectful distance. So naturally I grew up with a burning desire to find my way to that centre, to outdo my countrymen through hard work and perseverance and to earn their admiration, if only grudging. Perhaps no such centre physically exists, but in my mind it was represented by that city, and in my chosen profession, by that man.

I have no intention of talking about myself beyond what is relevant to this story, but I offer this information in an attempt to explain why it was so particularly horrible for me to be banished to the provinces for my apprenticeship, and why Mezzanotte stood out as a beacon of hope during those long years. My fear was that I would get bogged down out there, that some provincial doctor would want to marry me or, worse, that I would want to marry him. If I had his child, I would be lost for ever. So I kept my eyes on that beacon and I told myself that as soon as I had served my time, he would light my way back to the centre. And so he did.

Ever since I answered that advertisement and went to work for Mezzanotte for the first time, his summonses had punctuated my life like a series of flashbulbs in the dark, giving it meaning and shape. My life before that advertisement receded from me in an indistinct blur; the people to whom I had been close had, in the natural course of things, faded away. The only constant in my life now was my work at the hospital; that was my lifeblood, and the source of it, the warm beating heart, was Mezzanotte. As soon as one project ended, I looked forward to the next. He called these projects my real work and that's what they were to me. The rest, as interesting as I found it, was killing time.

Now here we were again, about to embark on a new project.

Together, the professor and I would bring Patient DL back into the world. Her family would be grateful to us, as would she, and we would publish another paper which would enter the archive, setting a precedent for future cases of its kind and earning us both a little more respect, a little more fame. Or we would ascertain that there was nothing left of her, the machines would be switched off and the bed freed up for a patient with a better chance of life. Either way we couldn't fail. The whole experiment lay in front of us, another thrilling adventure, so why couldn't I just abandon myself to it as usual?

I couldn't. Ever since my visit to Mezzanotte the day before, when I had gazed down on an old man, a doubt had hovered at the back of my mind. It occurred to me then, with a painful shock, that one day he would simply stop calling me; that I would have to go on alone, carving my lonely furrow in life. Here I was at last, at the centre of things, but what kind of a centre would it be without him? The prospect of life without Mezzanotte filled me with dread, and behind that idea was another one; a fear almost too nebulous to grasp. I can't put my finger on it, except to say that it had to do with knowing that people don't just vanish like that. It rarely happens that one minute they are here, their old selves, and the next they're gone. More often they change, slowly at first and then beyond all recognition. Finally they peter out, so that if you blinked you might miss their sorry little expiration.

As a distant clock chimed eleven, I heard the door to the chapel open again. A moment later the chaplain in scuffed leather jacket and dog collar came into view, moving across the central space towards the pulpit. A young man, with straight fair hair that stuck up at the back, he carried a motorbike helmet in one hand and a pair of leather gloves in the other. Catching sight of me, his eyes lit up and he hurried over. 'Hello!' he said, as I rose to my feet. 'What can I do for you?'

I answered as I always did: 'Nothing, thank you. I was just leaving.'

He looked crestfallen, so I told him that I found his chapel a good place to think. What's more, judging by the traffic through there that morning, other people also came there when they had difficult matters to resolve. 'They do?' he said, and looked even sadder. Then he forced a smile and assured me that I was welcome to drop in any time. He was always there to 'lend an ear'. I thanked him again and left.

8

It only remained for me to make the practical arrangements. Nestor, for some reason, did not like to use the telephone, but I knew that he was usually to be found by the signpost around five thirty in the afternoon. He surfaced four or five times a day from his subterranean lair to smoke on the front steps (all smoking was obviously prohibited on the premises), then slipped back down through the unmarked door. But at five thirty he lingered, because it was then – just before supper – that the nurses changed shifts.

You could see him there, rocking backwards and forwards on the balls of his feet, hands in pockets, head lowered, discreetly inspecting the girls from beneath his eyelids, fixing his gaze on their calves and raising it slowly to the little watches pinned to their breasts. This was where I found him when I wanted to arrange the transfer of the equipment to the fifth floor.

We agreed a time of three o'clock the following afternoon. I was about to move off, not wishing to stay longer in his company than was necessary, when he laid a hand on my arm and brought his mouth close to my ear, so that I caught a whiff of stale tar. He understood the principle behind the professor's machine, he said, which was that the patient displaced the wave by brainpower alone, and that this simple action allowed her to communicate. He had seen the blueprints. What troubled him was this: he had made some enquiries, and had been reliably informed that DL was a vegetable. If that was so, and her brain was 'like porridge', then how could it displace anything? Why was the professor wasting their time, his own and ours?

'Not a vegetable,' I said, yanking my arm away, 'paralysed. And since you ask, porridge is the consistency of a healthy brain. Yours, for instance.' He looked suspicious, and I was about to elaborate when, over his shoulder, I caught the inquisitive glances of two nurses passing behind the signpost. 'Come on,' I said, 'I'll show you,' and for the second time in three days I followed him down into the basement. He pulled a second chair up to the table in his room, folded his forearms on the green baize, and watched intently as I scribbled on a sheet of paper. Snatching it away almost before I had completed the last stroke, he held it up to the light.

'Think of this as a roadblock,' I said, pointing with my pencil tip to the stylised base of the brain, at the point where it formed a junction with the spinal column. 'No traffic gets in or out. The control tower, up here, has lost contact with the troops, down here. That's putting it simplistically, of course.' Nestor laid the sheet down and jutted his stubbly chin over it. 'But here's the conundrum,' I went on, drawing a question mark inside the crude outline of a skull. 'Nobody knows what's going on *inside* the control tower. See? This here is a black box.'

He raised his head and looked at me with red-rimmed, calculating eyes. 'You mean, just because they're not transmitting, doesn't mean the generals aren't inside, peering out through binoculars, poring over their scale models, plotting and scheming as usual?'

I scratched my head with the end of the pencil. 'Well, sort of. Though . . .' and I paused, aware of the dangers of carrying an analogy too far. 'There's a chance they may also be lying dead on the floor, wiped out by a single grenade lobbed through an open window. We can't rule it out.'

Nestor nodded slowly, stroking his chin, and his lip curled into a sly smile, revealing a single yellow canine. 'Well, well, the old devil,' he said. 'So what are the odds?' I told him there was no way of knowing until we put her to work on the machine. With a look of what I took to be approval, he bent over the diagram again.

The next day I made sure I arrived in Diane's room ahead of the appointed time. Her head lolled on the pillow, her slack features were bathed in the bright electric light, but as I entered a spasm seized the muscles of her lips and twitched them out into something that resembled a joyful smile. Already that smile had lost its charm for me and I saw in it something enslaved and robotic. It was strange how immune I had become to it, just through knowing how it came about. Nevertheless I squeezed her hand and explained to her what was about to happen. Taking up a position by the window, I crossed my arms over my chest and waited for Nestor. He arrived with a toolbox and an assistant, one of the junior porters. The boy, who had acne and a slouch, pushed a trolley with the equipment on it: the sinister-looking grey boxes and the computer monitor whose screen was temporarily blank. Both of them wore blue overalls and I watched their faces closely as they entered.

The boy's expression altered as soon as he saw Diane. His eyebrows shot up and he turned to me with a questioning look. Nestor kept his eyes carefully averted. He put his toolbox down on the chair and rummaged about in it. Then he went to work, whistling as he did so, casting the occasional covert glance at me or at the patient, whose face was once more devoid of expression. He didn't say a word, except to give orders to his assistant, or to explain to me how a particular switch or gadget worked. After an hour, each of the grey modules and the computer monitor was bolted on to a hinged bracket on the wall over the bed, but in such a way as not to interfere with the other, life-monitoring machinery that was already there. At last the two of them filed out of the room, the boy casting a hopeful backward glance in the direction of the bed.

As soon as they were gone I glared at my pupil. The way she smiled at those two had been almost flirtatious. The way Nestor avoided her eye as he danced around the bed, raising and lowering his arms, adorning the wall behind her, was like some kind of grotesque courtship dance. I glared at her, then in spite of myself I felt my gaze soften. I couldn't blame her for what was no more than a cruel joke played on her by her synapses. The fault was mine, for having exposed her to the inquisitive looks of strangers. Now, down in the bowels of the hospital, they would be talking about her, speculating, laughing obscenely. Feeling pity for the poor, defenceless creature, I turned abruptly away and, clasping my hands behind my back, studied the wall that was covered with photos, letters and drawings.

One of the photos in particular interested me. It showed a young woman with long dark hair drawn back into a ponytail, holding a palette smeared with coloured paint and smiling into the camera. Diane, of course, in the days before her accident. Behind her I saw a large room with wooden floorboards, a skylight in steeply sloping eaves and in the corner, a narrow bed. Besides this there was very little furniture, just an easel and stool, some canvases stacked against a wall, and at the foot of the bed, a small statue that seemed to be made from bronze or possibly a dark wood.

I couldn't take my eyes off that picture. It fascinated me in the same way that pictures of the dead fascinate the living, even if they never knew them. At a footstep behind me I started and turned to see Mezzanotte sweep through the doorway, a rain-spotted green Loden draped over his shoulders, his thick white hair dampened and swept back from his forehead. He stopped just short of the bed, peeling off his black leather gloves, smiling uncertainly, even a little self-consciously, at its occupant.

'It's a reflex,' I said, quickly. 'She smiles like that at everyone.'

The smile vanished and he threw her a reproachful look. Then his eye fell on the components of his machine, discreetly arranged on the wall around Diane's bed, and his face lit up again. He barely seemed to notice the other objects in the room, the clutter on the sideboard, the flower-filled vases, the papier mâché wall. Removing his coat, he walked around the bed in front of me, flung it over the back of the rocking chair and took a seat, draping his gloves over his knee. Then, with a 'Please', and an elegant sweep of his arm, he indicated that I should begin the demonstration.

I went to work. The first step was to prop the patient up on the pillow (she was light but tall, or rather long, and limp as an oyster), clamp her head into the vertical support and lower the cap of electrodes over her forehead. I talked as I did so, explaining why I was doing such-and-such, letting her know it wouldn't hurt. Mezzanotte sat forward in the chair, cupping his chin artfully between thumb and forefinger, one leg bent back beneath him and the other pointing forward, as if he too were paying court. I pulled out the computer monitor on its bracket and swung it into place in front of her face. Then I glanced at him. He was gazing at Diane with such longing in his dark eyes that I felt a little pang of jealousy. It passed, and I realised there was something peculiar about that look: it was as if he were making a wish, or offering up a prayer to her. Pleading with her to cooperate and promising her riches if she did. At last he tore his eyes away and nodded to me to indicate that he was ready to proceed.

Addressing my subject I explained the rules of the game, simple as they were, and suggested possible images she could use: Mezzanotte's ringmaster, Nestor's traffic lights, even something as simple as electricity accumulating in a rain cloud. As long as it contained the notion of a build-up of pressure to some kind of breaking point, at which another action would be triggered, it could be helpful to her. I was careful to stress that each individual had to find his or her own strategy, and that what worked for one person might not work for another. I glanced over my shoulder at Mezzanotte, saw that he was looking at me thoughtfully, even in admiration, and blushed.

Once my preparations were complete, I pressed a button so that the apple and pear appeared on the screen, indicated the line she should try to disrupt and sat down on the wooden chair. I tried to sit very still, on the assumption that she was working and so as not to break her concentration, and I kept my eyes on the screen. At one point, aware of a movement behind the monitor, I glanced at the professor and saw that his head had jerked up. He had dozed off and woken himself with the movement. It was warm in the room and a moment later his head had fallen on to his chest again. His mouth gaped, he snored gently. 'Professor,' I hissed, irritated at having to break my rule of silence. He didn't hear me, and gazing helplessly at the lined face, the flaccid cheeks and the lips, slightly parted, which twitched in sleep, I marvelled at the changes old age had already wrought in him. A wave of fatigue came over me then, and sinking back in my chair I let my own eyelids droop. Silence spread out in the room, broken only by the electrical hum of the machinery, and in my half-dozing state I imagined that the three of us were in the same boat: old people growing older in a room where it was always mid-afternoon, and where the blinds had been drawn to keep out the sun. I sat up, wide awake, and called to Mezzanotte again. He snored on, I couldn't reach him until, in agitation, I shouted, 'Wake up!'

'What? Who?' he slurred, lurching forward in the chair and looking wildly around him.

I explained again, patiently, that the lesson had ended. He immediately wanted to know if I had recorded any change in the signal. So I had to remind him that it was only the first attempt. It was too early to expect a response. He couldn't hide his disappointment. A moment later he gave me a piercing look and asked me if I had a feeling about this patient. Did I detect a life force, a will to fight? I thought for a minute. I wanted to say yes, to tell him about the look of contempt I had seen on the very first day, which Fleur Bartholomew thought I had imagined. But under his burning gaze something prevented me, and I replied instead that I couldn't say. Anger flared in his eyes, then died. He got to his feet, balanced his coat on his shoulders and made his way around the bed, pausing to peer at the photo of the artist in her studio, which somehow drew all eyes past the other amateur offerings pasted up around it. Suddenly he let out a loud yelp of laughter and spun round to gape at the patient, his coat fanning out around him. 'What is it?' I cried, alarmed. He looked at me, blinking in surprise, then crossed the room in a few rapid steps and laid his hand on my shoulder as I rose towards him. Holding my breath, I waited for his explanation, but he just beamed down at me with that astonished expression, patted my shoulder and turned away. In the doorway, he gazed back at the patient. Then he was gone.

With a sigh, I began to dismantle the equipment, the voice

of the TV presenter babbling away in my ear. At one point something she said caught my attention and I glanced up. The topic under discussion was the restoration of Michelangelo's David, but it was only when the image of the statue appeared on the screen that my interest was really piqued and I perched on the end of the bed to listen. A reporter was explaining that David had for centuries stood as a symbol of physical perfection. But a closer look . . . and here the camera zoomed in on various parts of the statue's anatomy . . . revealed that its fabric had taken a certain amount of abuse. Where the lower half of the left arm had been broken off by rioting mobs and fitted with a new one sometime in the last century, the join had been visible because of the different chemical make-up of the two pieces of marble. But, the reporter explained, the restorers had cleverly hidden it using their sophisticated techniques. They had also managed to repair a toe on the left foot, which had been smashed by a madman armed with a hammer, and had covered up some other damage caused by lightning.

An art historian came on to say that he didn't hold with restoration, because the greatest works of art were produced by more than one artist anyhow, over long periods of time, and each epoch had its own idea of beauty. Even if it was the work of a single individual, which was rare, the true artist intended his works to age gracefully. 'A work of art is pretty much like a human being,' he said. 'We get battered, we break bones, they mend, we go and get some disease, it's cured, we die.'

It was then that something fell into place in my mind. I got up from the bed and crossed the room to the wall where the photograph was pasted. The statuette at the foot of the bed was, of course, a miniature reproduction of David. The professor must have recognised it instantly.

Glancing surreptitiously over my shoulder, I was surprised to see that Diane's gaze was riveted to the TV. A tear that had formed in the corner of her eye was spilling over on to her cheek. She was still wearing the pink plastic helmet, which gave her a forlorn, doll-like appearance. The televised discussion had caught my attention before I had had a chance to remove it, she had slumped down the bed a little and her head had fallen to one side. Still her eyes didn't waver from the screen. Horrified, I ran to wipe away the tear that had now splashed on to her cheek. Peeling off the helmet, I smoothed her hair back from her forehead and laid her down flat, pulling the coverlet up over her chest. 'There,' I murmured. 'Don't cry.'

Now she was horizontal and her line of vision had swung up from the television so that she gazed at a point just below the ceiling. Still the tears welled up in her eyes, and patiently, with my own handkerchief, I wiped them away. It's just the excess of electricity in her nervous system, I told myself, which in turn is leading to overstimulation of the lachrymal gland. The tears flow over the cornea, lubricate the conjunctiva and drain out through those pinpricks in the eyelids, the tear ducts. The machinery is still in excellent working order. It is possible that she saw the images on the TV, or heard the words of the presenter, and understood. It's possible that they tapped a buried memory and released a spring of sadness, or joy. But any link between the memory banks and the tear ducts was probably severed at the time of her accident – so in all likelihood, the timing of her tears is a coincidence. Nothing more.

That is what I told myself. But still the tears continued to flow, running down her cheeks in two narrow rivulets. Seated beside her, I dabbed first at the right cheek, then at the left; the right cheek then the left. I sang to her, the first nursery rhyme that came to mind, 'Humpty Dumpty sat on a wall . . .', in a vain attempt to jolt the defective nervous system out of its loop. I cooed into her ear with the same idea. But it was no good, the tears kept coming and soon my handkerchief was soaked through. Reluctantly, I got up to leave. I had patients to see. When I looked back from the doorway, the spontaneous tears were still streaming down her face, seeping into the pillowcase and pooling in the hollow at the base of her throat.

9

The first few lessons all passed off without the patient offering any response or sign of life. That is, no meaningful sign of life. For the first few days I saw nothing of her relatives, but I knew that Dr Bartholomew had asked them to keep their distance, just until I had established a routine. On the fourth day I arrived a little earlier than usual, just before ten, and found an old man sitting by the bed. He had his back to me, his long yellowish-white hair flowed over his shoulders and he seemed to be admonishing some invisible creature at his feet. 'That's enough now,' he muttered. 'No more fooling around.'

I crept up behind him and saw that the creature was Diane's hand. He was massaging it tenderly, and it lay against his large, lined palm: a tiny, translucent claw. 'It's not nice,' he murmured, 'teasing your old dad like that.'

I cleared my throat and he turned his head, so that I saw his pale blue eyes which bulged above his cheekbones. 'Who is it?' he demanded, and I realised he was blind. I introduced myself, he relaxed a little and told me that he was John Wraith,

Diane's father. He lumbered to his feet, a great bear of a man with a prominent forehead and a grizzled white chin. 'Have you brought the machine?' he asked, and stooping a little, twisting his head to left and right, flared his nostrils at me. 'It must be very small.'

I explained that the machine was already there, in the room around him. He drew in his neck, blinked several times and asked me to describe it. I did so, and then I explained how it tapped into a kind of brainwave we called a slow cortical potential, a form of energy really, how it used this energy to pick out letters from the alphabet, how the energy could be trained . . .

As I spoke he coughed and smiled a pitying smile. When I stopped talking he turned towards the foot of the bed, so that I was presented with his three-quarter profile, and looked intently at a spot on the floor. I started to speak again, but he raised a finger to his lips. Behind him now, I could see Diane's head lying obliquely across the pillow. Her eyes were half closed, her lips parted in a sardonic smile. It was quite different from the joyful smile that was her usual response to a new arrival, and yet it was equally familiar to me; her face took it on when devoid of all muscle tension – that was its resting state, so to speak. I glanced back at the old man, who had strayed further towards the foot of the bed. He was standing stock-still, his head cocked towards the window as if he were listening to a bird singing in the garden. It occurred to me that it would be easy to believe that she were communicating some idea to him, but at a frequency out of the normal range. I couldn't hear it, but perhaps an elephant could, or a blind man. The apparent coincidence of their actions amused me. Diane's smile faded just as the old man raised his head. He mumbled something, I didn't catch it, and turning back to me he announced that my pupil was ready for her lesson.

He asked courteously if he should leave. I told him that he would have to go for the lesson itself, that was my rule, but he could stay while I assembled the equipment. He stood at the foot of the bed, his fingers curled lightly round the bar, his head resting on his hunched shoulders, listening. When it came to adjusting the vertical clamp, I turned the screw slowly. As I did so, I noticed that he was becoming agitated. A frown rippled across his forehead, he ground his teeth and tightened his grip on the bar. Experimentally, I loosened the screw a few turns. His forehead became smooth again, his grip relaxed. I repeated the process, tightening and then loosening the vice, and he became agitated and calm exactly in sync with my actions. I tightened the screw by one more turn than I had dared to before, not so far as to hurt her, but perhaps to cause her a mild discomfort, and provoked a furious 'Easy!' from the old man. I quickly loosened it off and asked him, straight out, if he had a way of knowing how Diane was feeling.

John Wraith pursed his lips and directed his viscous glare at the counterpane, at the small hillock formed by her feet. He was breathing noisily through his nostrils, which flared with each exhalation. When his breathing returned to normal, he moved around to the far side of the bed, trailing the knuckles of his right hand along the counterpane, and standing by her head, hooked his right forefinger to beckon me closer. I approached from my side and, following his lead, bent over the bed. As I did so, Diane's eyeballs rolled up smartly into her head, leaving the whites grotesquely exposed. Involuntarily I gasped. 'Games . . .' he murmured, and I glanced sharply up at him. Had he seen? Surely not. His milky-blue eyes roved from left to right, as if scanning a page of a book. Then he called her softly by name. 'Watch,' he whispered to me.

I trained my gaze on her face and to my astonishment, became aware of dozens of tiny movements under the skin. The muscles around her eyes and mouth seemed to be quivering. From only a short distance away these tiny movements cancelled each other out, so that the effect was that of a sometimes slack, sometimes rigid, but always expressionless mask. Close up I could see that this was an illusion. Those muscles were in a constant state of flux. It was like watching the surface of a trout pool teeming with fish.

'Diane,' the old man cooed again. Now his eyes were fixed on her face, and they glowed with the intense, predatory concentration of a fisherman who knows his pool. Under this blazing spotlight her face seemed to melt and run like wax. The eyebrows rose and the muscles at the corners of her eyes tautened. A sound came from her throat, a strangled chuckle. In the depths of her eyes, a light burned.

'There,' the old man breathed, his leonine muzzle hovering over her, his breath stirring a strand of hair on her forehead. 'There . . .'

10

The following day I met Mrs Wraith. It happened by chance, since I had already finished my lesson, packed up the equipment and returned to my office. Some time later, I realised I had mislaid the card that identified me as an employee of the hospital. Thinking it must have fallen out of my pocket during Diane's lesson, I took advantage of a five-minute break between patients to hurry back up to the fifth floor.

A woman turned away from the window as I stepped over the threshold of Diane's room, letting go of the curtain she had been gripping between her long, ivory fingers. The anxiety clouding her features gave way to a smile, and she crossed the room towards me.

'You must be Dr Newman,' she said, holding out her hand. 'Denise Wraith.'

She took my hand firmly and held it for a long time, scanning my face with her dark eyes. Perhaps I imagined it, but minutes seemed to pass before she finally pronounced, 'My daughter is going to like you.'

I could say nothing, so struck was I by the resemblance

between her and the patient. Both had the same dark hair, cropped short, though hers was coarser and threaded with silver. Both had the same dark eyes, though she had accentuated the slant of hers with eyeliner. The shape of the face, oval with a small nose and strong chin, was identical. The mother's mouth was painted a deep crimson, and lines of pain or disappointment drew it down at the outer corners towards the powdered point of her chin. Her cheeks which were dashed with rouge high up on the zygoma melted into pale jowls below. She was still striking to look at, and elegant. She must once have been slender, too, but with age she had thickened around the neck, around the waist and hips. This extra bulk she carried off, for the most part, thanks to the vigour of her movements and her height (she must have been only a little shorter than her giant of a husband). She wore a white blouse tucked into a pair of black trousers which were drawn in at the waist by a wide belt. A double string of lacquered wooden beads hung down between her generous breasts. The girl, by contrast, wore a simple white shift, out of which her bare limbs poked like tent poles that might be carried away on the wind at any moment. I put the mother in her late fifties, but looking from one to the other of them, it seemed to me that it wasn't age that separated them. It was as if a sculptor had created two identical statues, put one on public display, exposed to the elements, and the other away in a dark cupboard for his own viewing pleasure.

'Your daughter takes after you,' I said at last.

'Not just in looks,' she replied, with a smile.

She let go of my hand. I explained why I had come and

she said she would help me search for the missing pass. Immediately she got down on her knees and started energetically waving her arms under the bed, talking all the time, while I stood letting my eye rove over the room. She had so much been looking forward to meeting me, she said, there was so much to tell me about the terrible things that went on in this hospital. At that she sat back on her haunches and wrinkled her nose.

'Something is rotten in this place. Don't you think so?'

'I'm not sure,' I said, cautiously. 'What do you mean?'

She shook her head. She couldn't put her finger on it. First there was the building itself. It was gloomy and that was bad for morale among the longer-term patients. Plus it wasn't well signposted. You could easily get lost in it. The staff were underpaid and overworked, which meant there was a fast turnover, and the nurses who looked after Diane didn't have time to form an attachment to her. She suspected them of handling her roughly and, perhaps, of stealing her things. Then there were the lifts, not to mention all the other machinery, which was old. The cameras they used to 'take pictures' inside Diane's head immediately after her accident were outdated even then.

'It's scandalous,' she said, and shook her head.

If the cameras had been up-to-date, she went on, the doctors might have been able to pinpoint exactly what was broken and mend it, just as she sat here by the bedside and sewed on the buttons that got torn off her daughter's clothes in the hospital laundry. Diane might have been up and about years ago. But cameras like that cost money, and money was short. The country was overstretched, taxes were being funnelled into the prime minister's pet projects, on new government buildings, on wars in countries no one had heard of . . . She went very pale, took a deep breath and continued in a low voice. Meanwhile, this place rotted from the inside out. 'It's like an old woman. Made comfortable, mothballed.' Her voice shook as she uttered these last words.

Just then, to my relief, I discovered the missing pass balanced on a corner of the sideboard. When I held it up she looked momentarily disappointed. I explained, apologetically, that I couldn't stay.

'Of course not,' she replied, raising herself up with some effort from her kneeling position. 'The world can't stop for one patient, can it?' I looked at her uncertainly. She laughed, a warm, honeyed laugh that showed her strong, white, even teeth, and waved me away. 'Run along!' she said. 'There'll be plenty of time for us to get to know each other later.'

I saw her the next day too. It was her habit, as I knew from the nurses, to arrive soon after I had gone and to stay for a couple of hours. That day, and in fact often over the weeks to come, she arrived a little ahead of time, while I was still packing up. For the first few minutes she wouldn't utter a word, she wouldn't even acknowledge my presence, but would wander up and down the room, apparently aimlessly. I busied myself with the equipment until such time as she was ready to talk to me. Then she would greet me with a 'Hello!', as if I had only just walked into the room, or she had only just noticed me. After that we would chatter away like old acquaintances.

I was puzzled by that silent interlude that preceded each

of our daily conversations, and I tried to explain it by telling myself that she was interested in watching me work, but didn't wish to disturb the proceedings or to distract her daughter's attention. So one day I tried to reassure her: 'We can chat while I put things away, you know. I don't mind, because by then the lesson is over.' She looked at me with a blank expression and turned to gaze at the window.

As the days passed it occurred to me that perhaps this odd behaviour of hers had nothing to do with me. I decided to watch her more closely and I quickly saw that there was nothing aimless about her activity in those few minutes. She would stride into the room carrying her basket, which was heavy, judging by the way she swung it on to the floor by the rocking chair, and the faint expiration that escaped her as she released it. Then she would cross the room to the sideboard, to the end nearest the television and the door, and the ritual would commence.

I should explain that even at that time, early on in our experiment, the sideboard was littered with gifts that Denise herself brought, day after day: toys designed to stimulate a baby's senses, scented candles, baubles, dried flowers, magazines, chocolates, fruit. She brought them in the basket and arranged them along the ledge, but it was the nurses who, on her say-so, removed the perishables in armfuls when the time came – the magazines unread, the fruit uneaten.

The offerings did not arrive randomly, as the fancy took her, but they replaced others now vanished. This much I deduced from observing her, discreetly, from beneath lowered eyelids. One day in particular I remember, because it was the first day she broke her self-imposed silence ahead of time. Then, as she did every day, she moved slowly along the sideboard, sometimes with her hands folded behind her back, sometimes letting them flutter over the objects arranged there. Pausing by a bowl of coloured cotton reels, frowning, she ran her fingers through it. 'One is missing,' she muttered, 'or is it two . . . ?' Then she moved off again, still keeping close to the sideboard. Her hand brushed over some green apples in a bowl and I noticed that her pale fingers trembled slightly. When she reached the window she gripped a pleat in the curtain and turned her head this way and that, looking down into the garden, scanning the windows in the opposite side of the wing, interrogating the leaden, wintry sky.

Hurrying back to the bowl of cotton reels, she began feverishly to count through them a second time. Then, turning to face the room, she solemnly announced that the thief had struck again. I straightened up, feigning surprise. I asked her what kind of person would steal a bit of thread from a paralysed woman. She smiled and fixed me with her weary gaze. 'A very ordinary person could be tempted to steal,' she said, 'even if they had no need for the object in question, just because it was lying there, within reach, and they thought nobody was watching.'

I asked her if the objects couldn't simply have been misplaced, moved in dusting or borrowed, but she shook her head. The thieving had been going on systematically for a few months now, and it seemed to her no coincidence that it had started around the time that Adrian Levy had first, as she put it, 'threatened' her daughter's life. Almost every day something went missing: a photograph, a liqueur chocolate, a joker from a pack of playing cards. Always something small and insignificant so only she noticed its absence. She imagined that it had become a compulsion on the part of the thief, a sort of ritual, because the objects themselves had little or no intrinsic value. She was afraid that word might have spread through the hospital, that it might have become entertainment for a ring, a circle of reprobates who got their kicks from tormenting patients and their families. Sometimes, lying awake at night, she was haunted by a vision of anonymous hordes roaming through the hospital, looking in at each door, their greedy eyes alighting on her daughter's grinning, helpless face. But in another way, a very strange way, she had come to rely on the thefts. Her eyes filled with tears and she wiped one away with the back of her long, manicured hand. 'The worst days are the ones where I search and search, but I can't find what's missing.'

She sank down in the rocking chair and I crossed to the window, giving her time to compose herself. Beneath me the garden was empty, except for an old lady pushing a young man in a wheelchair. She was quite tall and angular, but trim and muscular as a gymnast, and she advanced slowly, pushing the chair and the obese young man slumped in it before her. Her smooth hair, swept up in a bun, was white as snow through the bare branches of a cherry tree.

Behind me Denise started talking again. Two days earlier she had asked that I call her by her first name. I pretended to have forgotten, preferring to keep a professional distance, but she was so insistent I had given in. Denise was telling me that she would happily move into the hospital if she could. Only then would she feel that her daughter was safe; that she could properly protect her. But the authorities wouldn't allow it, and besides, her husband was helpless without her.

'I thought he managed very well,' I said, turning back into the room.

'In the hospital, yes,' she replied, 'but outside, you should see him.' She laughed, a surprisingly harsh laugh. Yes, she went on, he was quite at home in the hospital now. But for the first few years after Diane's accident he barely left the house. That was when he was still losing his sight. Going blind was a *particular* tragedy for him, because he had relied so heavily on his eyes in his work. He had been an inventor.

'Oh?' I said, thinking of the old man as I had seen him on that first morning, and the almost mystical aura he seemed to carry with him. 'I would never have guessed.'

She smiled. 'No.'

Nevertheless he was good with his hands, he was green-fingered too, but above all his passion was for machines. Or 'gadgets', as she called them, dismissively. There was a time in his forties when he filed a patent almost every month. The most extraordinary and ingenious contraptions came out of his workshop. Then in his late fifties his eyes started to fail, just as his father's had before him and his father's before that. While he still had some vision left he sat inside all day, brooding. If she took him shopping or to a concert, and left him alone in a strange place for even a moment, he created a scene, shouting for her until she returned. Or else he would be bound to walk into some display or other, flail about and cause untold damage. In the end it was easier to leave him at home. It was only when the business with his eyes was finished and he could no longer tell whether it was night or day, that he agreed to visit his daughter. She hadn't been able to persuade him to until then. In the car on the way to the hospital he sat purse-lipped, staring grimly ahead. When they arrived she walked him round the place – she was afraid he would take fright at its echoing cavernousness, so she spoke to him gently and gave him time to get a feel for it. To her relief he took to it like a fish to water. He was still as clumsy as anything on the outside, but he could find his way about that hospital as if he had been born in it.

Suddenly her shoulders slumped and she sat very still. Then she roused herself and, leaning forward, drew a jar of butter-coloured cream from the basket at her feet. Rolling up her sleeves she scooped out a generous gob, picked up Diane's wrist with her other hand and began to smear it into the delicate hand and forearm. 'Skin and bone,' she muttered, with a click of her tongue. 'It wasn't always that way, though, was it, love?'

I had taken advantage of her brief trance to move towards the door, but I paused and glanced back at her. She gave a deep and sorrowful sigh, modulated by her own vigorous movements as she worked the glutinous substance into the lifeless arm. My curiosity aroused, I sidled back towards her and asked her if Diane had had more flesh on her at some time during her stay in the hospital.

'Oh!' she cried, and chuckled into her double chin. About seven years ago, she said, for about a year, I wouldn't have recognised the girl lying in that bed. That was a difficult time. To cut a long story short, her daughter's husband had all but barred her from the hospital. He wanted to care for his wife himself, he said, and she had gone along with his wish for a time, because she could see that he was still grieving. After she had kept her distance for six months, she turned up at the hospital one day. She came at an hour when she knew he would be working, quite simply, to check up on her daughter.

When she arrived in the room, her first impression was of having entered a much smaller room than she remembered, a nursery or child's bedroom with a very low ceiling. Then she saw why. Diane had grown obese. In the space of only six months, she had been utterly transformed. Her eyes had receded into her swollen face like apple pips, her chin had spilled over her chest and her inflated arms, taut as sausages, rolled over the side of the bed. 'She lay there like a beached whale,' she said, musingly.

She confronted Bartholomew, who had been too busy with other cases to attend properly to her daughter, and demanded that she call in a diabetes specialist. The specialist adjusted Diane's insulin and her weight began to recede. She asked a nurse why her daughter's hair had not been cut in months and lay in long, lank tendrils on the pillow, and the nurse told her that Mr Levy had prohibited anyone from trimming his wife's precious locks. The next day she brought in a pair of scissors and lopped it all off.

'What did your son-in-law have to say about that?' I asked.

She blinked at me, as if surprised to hear him described that way. She never found out what Levy thought about it, she said. He avoided her, and took to visiting at odd times of the day and night. He prowled around the hospital, coming close only when he knew the coast was clear. He probably stole to let them know he'd been there, though it was possible he paid others to do it for him, or others had merely seen and imitated him. Although she couldn't stop him, if only because this was a public building and a human being has to sleep sometimes, she made it clear he was trespassing on her territory now. She resumed her rightful place. She took up her vigil, watching over her daughter, and settled down to wait for the day when Diane would wake up; when, like Sleeping Beauty, she would sit up in bed and speak to her mother.

She smiled, a secret, knowing smile, and I realised that there was no doubt in her mind that day would come; nor that it would be her Diane wished to speak to first. I glanced back at the waif in the bed, whose large eyes dominating her sharp, elfin face, reminded me of nothing so much as one of those tiny nocturnal primates, a bushbaby, perhaps, or a marmoset. And who, though unable to move a muscle by her own free will, continued to surprise me.

11

We fell into a routine. Every morning I came in to find John Wraith murmuring over Diane's hands. Sometimes he would sing to her, a little off-key. But no matter how long he massaged the poor, twisted claws, they never loosened up. As soon as I had assembled the equipment he rose from his seat, retrieved his white stick and left.

I would wait for a minute, listening to the receding tap of his stick, before I began my lesson. A couple of minutes before the hour was up, Denise would arrive. While I dismantled the equipment, she placed her basket on the floor by the rocking chair and carried out her daily inspection. Her eyes with their dark, pencilled outlines and fine, concentric threads of fatigue would range fretfully over the papered wall, while her hands sought out the fruit, the glass paperweights, ran over the spines of the magazines, worried the beads of a tangle of cheap, costume jewellery, lifted the bottles of nail varnish and eventually came to rest on the curtain, a pleat of which she gripped tightly between her fingers. She stood for a few moments, scanning the garden and the facing windows. Only when she had completed this ritual would she unload the new delivery of gifts from her basket and distribute them about the sideboard. She talked as she did so, sometimes to me or sometimes, sotto voce, to her daughter. She spoke to Diane as people do to the very old or the very young, posing questions without waiting for a response, or answering them herself. Diane lay motionless under her sheet, her gaze sliding over the ceiling, a sardonic smile on her lips.

Weekends were different. It wasn't in my contract that I should work weekends, and when the first one came round I fully intended to take my quota of rest – if only to catch up on my backlog of paperwork. But on Saturday morning, as I stood in the shop beneath my flat in slippered feet, my head thick with sleep, waiting to pay for my bread and eggs, I happened to look at my watch and saw that it was time for Diane's lesson. It occurred to me that 'weekend' meant nothing to her, lying in her hospital room where temperature and light were maintained at constant levels, and that a regular routine was more important, especially while she was still learning.

So I hurried to let myself into my flat, dropped off the groceries, changed my slippers and left for the hospital. I came in the next day too, and after I had given Diane her lesson I stayed on to write up my logbook of the experiment. When Mr and Mrs Wraith arrived, I got up from the wooden chair and apologised for intruding on their family visit. But Denise was pleased I had come of my own accord and she asked me to stay and keep them company. I remarked that it was nice to see them together for once and she glanced at me like a startled deer in the forest. 'It's Sunday,' she said. 'We always come together on a Sunday.'

At their insistence, I resumed my task. I retreated to the window and wrote standing up, half turned towards the room. From there I had a full view of John Wraith who, further along the sideboard, was loading a large, flat bowl with clementines which he removed one by one from a paper bag. The expression on his face was one of grim absorption, as if he were trying hard to suppress the urge to sit down beside the bed, pick up the patient's hand and start to press out the knots in her muscles.

With great care he constructed a sturdy, square-based pyramid out of the fruit, feeling with both hands as he balanced one flattened, orange globe on top of the others. Meanwhile, across the room, his wife dominated the bed and the creature in it. On her orders a nurse brought a vase half-filled with water, which she placed on the bedside table. Then, laying a large bouquet on the counterpane, she went about unwrapping it. First she loosened the knot in the rough string with her long, tapering fingers, then she coaxed out the ends so that she could smooth out the paper without tearing it. She talked all the while, about how the winter was dragging on, about the endless building in the city, the dreary construction sites . . . Suddenly she broke off, and there was silence in the room. 'Lilies?' she asked, blinking down at the long stems lying in their unfurled paper.

The old man froze and grew pale. 'I asked for winter roses,' he said, turning towards her, offering her the palms of his hands like a white flag.

She pursed her lips and rebound the pale trumpets just as the florist had done. She handed the heavy bouquet to him, tapping his arm sharply with her right forefinger to warn him to receive it. 'These are not ours,' she said. Without a word he accepted the bundle, then stood there uncertainly, cradling it at arm's length like an unwanted orphan. Denise glided to the door, grasped his white stick which was propped in the corner there and, bringing it close to him, nudged his arm.

He took the stick and St Christopher-like, the bundle balanced in the crook of his right arm, moved towards the door. Pausing on the threshold, he twisted his head to listen. Denise had already seated herself by the bed and, humming, brought out her pot of ointment from the basket. Some emotion passed over his face, I saw it in the tautening of his muscles, and then he vanished. I pretended to pore over my notes. She struck up a monologue which she addressed to her daughter and I don't think she noticed when, a few minutes later, I slipped out too.

John Wraith was nowhere to be seen in the corridor, or in the space around the nurse's station, so he must have passed through there rapidly. When I reached the entrance hall I spotted him, a silhouette against the sky, dwarfed by the great portal that framed him and the stained-glass window with its symbols of ancient healing. He seemed a little unsteady on his feet, as if the hospital were a ship on a stormy sea. Beyond the opening the sky was grey and threatening. With his left hand he supported himself against the door frame, under the right arm he hugged the bouquet to his torso, while attempting with the same hand to manoeuvre his stick. The point of it hovered like an antenna over the steps that fell away beneath him. Finally he summoned up the courage to slide one foot down on to the first step, followed by the other, and in this way he gained the pavement. When I reached the door I saw him in the near distance, shuffling along, keeping close to the hospital wall. An ambulance careered into the square, siren blaring, and as it passed him he shrank into the wall, turning towards the sound so that I could see the terror in his face. I followed as, with tiny pigeon steps, he made his way through the cobbled passage and paused, cowering, where it emerged into the city beyond, his unseeing eyes raised to the dizzying skyline. The florist's was a short way down to his left. The pavements weren't crowded, it being Sunday, but one or two people passing him cast curious looks at the wretched, overgrown figure. Like a drowning man, John Wraith clung to the façades of the shops and houses that bordered the pavement, until he fell into the sanctuary of the flower shop and relinquished his bundle to the florist. How he recognised the shop, I couldn't say, unless he had counted out his own footsteps. But as soon as I came close myself, I realised how. Through the open doorway came the moist, earthy, scent-laden air of potted plants and cut flowers. I stood close to the window, watching him through it as, guided by the florist's hand, he sank down on to a bench against the wall. The florist went off to finish serving another customer and the old man sat patiently, his face deathly pale and perspiring, his breast heaving. Gradually, his breathing grew more regular, he flared his nostrils as if sampling the fragrant air and his mood seemed to lighten. A smile played about his lips and it occurred to me that he was trying to identify the different perfumes in the shop, perhaps even put names to them.

When the florist returned he raised his head and I heard him explain, apologetically, that lilies wouldn't do. He had chosen them for their marvellous scent, but his wife found them funereal. She insisted on winter roses. The florist disappeared into the back of the shop and returned with another bouquet. As the old man felt his way out of the shop, armed with it, I stepped forward. 'Can I help you?' I asked. He started, then his great paw shot out of his sleeve and found my forearm, his fingers resting lightly on it like a question. In reply I extended my elbow towards him, he gripped it more firmly and together we moved off towards the square.

After a minute or two, to make conversation, I asked him what he thought of our hospital. His face lit up. 'It's a good hospital,' he said. 'It grows like a plant.' I laughed and asked what he meant by that. He scratched his head, smiled self-consciously and said that he was mainly thinking of the plants that grew in the forest. As a young man he had made a study of them. Because not much light penetrated the forest canopy, they had to share out what little reached them, and the way they did it was ingenious. By some mechanism involving the transmission and reflection of rays, neither the leaves of a single plant nor those of neighbouring plants ever overlapped each other. The result was a highly regular, even symmetrical pattern of leaf growth that had struck him as beautiful, when he had been able to see it, and even now that it was no more than a memory. Similarly, the patients in the hospital seemed to arrange themselves by some mysterious mechanism, according to a simple rule: the higher you went, the sicker they were, and the more chronic or long-term the case, the further he or she was from the 'stalk' or the warm artery of the plant, that is, the nurse's station. You could tell how serious a case was just by which room it occupied. In his mind's eye, he saw the hospital as white and new; the rooms sunny and welcoming; the nurses always smiling. Under this gleaming surface, everything worked like clockwork – it was the epitome of an efficiently run system, just like a plant. Or a well-oiled machine. He added, almost shyly, 'I sometimes think the architect was blind.'

I smiled at the thought and we entered the cobbled alleyway. I knew that he knew where he was because he cocked his head to listen to the echo of our footsteps, his grip on my arm relaxed and a little of the tension seemed to go out of him. As we emerged into the light again I asked him if he considered his daughter a serious case, then, given the room she had been allocated. He thought about it. 'Yes and no,' he said, and his face hardened. 'I'm afraid my wife will be disappointed.'

I stopped, bringing him to a halt. 'Why do you say that?'

Pulling himself up to his full height, he frowned over my head into the mouth of the tunnel. According to him, his wife preferred not to believe the doctors, who said there was very little to be done for Diane, even in the best-case scenario. She held strongly to the possibility of a miracle; that her daughter would one day sit up, kick back her sheets and ask for her mother. His wife had been brought up by a father and brother who doted on her. The former was a politician, the latter a successful businessman. They were powerful men, so it was understandable that she assumed that if she wanted something badly enough, she would have it. That was the way she had been taught to look at the world. He saw it differently, he had his own ideas about what form the 'miracle' would take. Although his daughter was paralysed, her eyes were not. According to Dr Bartholomew, her vision was probably perfect. For a long time it had struck him as ironic, cruel even, that he was blind but had all his limbs, while his daughter found herself in the opposite predicament. But then, gradually, he realised that there was a reason for this strange symmetry. Separately they were flawed, together they were whole. Some people donated organs to their children, but perhaps that wasn't always necessary. You could live symbiotically in other ways; you could live closely, in the same house, and coordinate your activities. You could learn to read one another's desires and intentions. You could become fused in spirit, while remaining bodily separate. He smiled, and his milky-blue eyes watered in the breeze.

I took his arm again and we moved on to the hospital. When we reached the steps I started to count them out for him. He interrupted me, saying he knew exactly how many there were. He seemed in a rush to get inside and once he was there he let go of my arm, hurrying towards the lifts with a tap-tap of his stick against the slate floor. I followed more slowly, marvelling at my own new understanding of what it was to be blind. It was gloomy in the entrance hall, as usual, but John Wraith imagined himself moving through a white, sunlit space; a gleaming sanctuary where passers-by smiled at him and meant him well. Just then, my eyes picked out the white of the signpost and I stopped, staring. Nestor leaned against it, half turned away from me. He was holding some object whose outer covering he seemed to peel off with his free hand before raising it to his lips. A liqueur chocolate, perhaps. His hands dropped to his sides and the object melted away. Perhaps he had swallowed it, or perhaps I had imagined it. Anyhow, he moved off towards the door that led to the basement, and vanished through it.

When I caught up with Wraith, he stood patiently in front of the closed doors of one of the two lifts, his large hands resting on the handle of his white cane and his head bowed. With his great height and the floral offering tucked lightly under his arm, he looked like the guardian of the entrance to a tomb, the Pharaoh's faithful servant whose function it was to prevent outsiders from ascending to the royal apartments. A few paces away the second lift stood with its doors open, waiting to receive passengers. When I pointed it out to him, he turned slightly towards me. 'Something's worn in this one,' he said. Then he turned back and bowed his head again, and I realised that he was listening to the grinding mechanism as the ancient lift descended in fits and starts.

12

One evening around the end of February I was working late, when I glanced over my shoulder at the lights across the wing. Some impulse, I can't say what it was, drew me to my feet, propelled me along through the series of rooms that housed me and my assistants and up to the fifth floor. As the lift doors opened, I saw that the nurse had temporarily abandoned her station. I slipped past it into the long corridor, which was lit in night mode. Sounds of rhythmic breathing came from the rooms and mingled in the corridor, where only the low lighting guided my footsteps. The faint red glow of the life-preserving machinery splashed the bare wall facing the doorways, so that I had the unpleasant sensation of moving through a womb.

When I turned in at Diane's door it took my eyes a moment to adjust to the scene. There was only a small night light on in a panel over her bed, but I was able to discern that a second figure lay stretched out beside her. Slim, fitting easily into the third or quarter of the bed left free at her side, I made out that he wore combat trousers, a leather jacket and a hood over his head. His thin arm circled the waist of the patient who lay flat on her back, motionless, like a mummy. The sheet was pushed down to her ankles and the figure was writhing against her bare thigh over which her shift was rucked up.

'Stop!' I shouted. 'Stop that!'

Electrified, the creature leapt into the air, landed on his toes and zigzagged across the room towards me. I raised my arms to block his escape but he ducked and was through, streaking down the corridor towards the bend and beyond to the illuminated reception area. I rocked back on my heels, hung there in dumb shock, murmured, 'I'm dreaming,' then snapped to my senses and ran off in pursuit.

As the nurse's station appeared up ahead of me, still with no sign of the nurse, I saw the door to the stairwell behind the lifts slowly closing and followed the intruder in. His steps were soundless but each time I glanced down into the well I caught sight of his dark, tousled head from which the hood had fallen back, spinning round several floors beneath me. Occasionally I heard the squeak of his palm against the banister as he pulled himself round a corner. The door to the basement closed with a thud and I was seized with an awful premonition: that he was going to find Nestor's room and destroy our equipment.

I threw myself down the remaining stairs and burst through the heavily sprung basement door, encountering pitch black. Groping for a switch I found one that lit up a small square of the panelled ceiling above my head. It was enough to see by and I ran, my stomach constricting as I noticed the strip of light under Nestor's door. I pushed it open and there he was, the intruder, one buttock resting lightly on the little folding card table, one foot encased in a battered desert shoe dangling beneath it, his long, bronzed and darkly bearded face turned towards me. He was in his mid-thirties, and I knew him immediately: Adrian Levy.

'Good evening,' he said, as if he had been sitting there for minutes, waiting for me. The only clue to his recent exertion was the glitter in his dark eyes. Outraged, struggling to catch my breath, I demanded to know how he had got into the hospital, and by what authority he had gained access to this room. 'No-one's,' he said, with a shrug. Then he got up from the table, walked round behind it and jabbed with his index finger at the wooden cross hanging on the wall, so that it tilted on its nail. 'My alter ego must be making his rounds,' he said, 'or he would have locked the door.'

I shuddered. I couldn't help it. He saw it and smiled. Turning back to the little wooden cross that he had just unbalanced, he put up two hands to right it. As he did so he enquired casually, throwing the question over his shoulder, if I knew what he did for a living.

'How should I?' I asked, annoyed.

'Journalist for the *Post*,' he replied. 'Lately, war correspondent. Eastern sector.'

He moved across the back of the room now and bending over, his hands folded behind him, peered down at a mess of well-thumbed magazines scattered on the floor in the corner. He stooped to pick one up: a catalogue of computer accessories. He examined the cover, then the back, and glanced at me over the top of it with his bright eyes. He'd just come back from the front, he said. He called it the front, even though officially one wasn't supposed to refer to the war as a war. It was a peacekeeping operation. Things were deteriorating over there, and they would get worse before they got better. The hotel he and the other reporters were put up in was shelled daily. Most of the Americans and the British had been forbidden to leave it. His editor, who fortunately valued life cheaply, had given him carte blanche to cover any story in the city. He had been close to the front line, close enough to watch the missiles strike. He had been out into the camps with his translator. There were two attempts to kidnap them, one to blow him up. He had survived and returned to tell the tale. 'I'm a hero,' he said, with a crooked smile.

I glared at him. 'You're trespassing.'

Tossing the magazine back on to the floor, he let out a sigh – of exasperation, perhaps, or disgust. Then he sauntered towards me with the easy grace of the very fit, stopping just a few centimetres from me. He smelt of hot dust and diesel. His eyes ran lightly over my hair and face. 'I expected a man,' he said.

I continued to glare at him, but now I felt the blood rise into my neck and cheeks. 'Don't worry,' he said bitterly, and his breath was cool on my cheek. 'No intercourse took place. No intercourse of any kind. What you interrupted just now was the emotional reunion of a dead man with his wife. Or, if you prefer, a man with his dead wife.'

Then he was striding past me to the door.

'Where are you going?' I gasped, turning round.

'Your office,' he called back over his shoulder. He was already some way ahead of me by the time I stepped out into the corridor, moving quickly past the stacks of obsolete computers. We climbed the staircase and strode, Indian file, across the darkened entrance hall, which was bound by four equidistant points of light: the stained-glass window above the door, and the accumulated glow of the lights lining each of the three corridors: those leading to the juvenile and geriatric wings, and to the north wing. I had to run to keep up and our dissonant footsteps echoed around the high ceiling. We headed for the north wing, but Levy shunned the lifts. He took the stairs three at a time, he seemed to know his way around. When he arrived at the entrance to my suite he stood back to wait for me, making a low bow as I flew past him, panting, my key in my outstretched hand.

As soon as the room was lit and we were seated, me behind my desk, he comfortable in the armchair where I put new patients at their ease, one mud-streaked boot poised on the opposite knee, his hands clasped behind his head, I asked him what he had meant by calling Nestor his alter ego.

'Only that while I risk life and limb on the other side of the continent, my mother-in-law believes I stalk the hospital every night, unpicking her embroidery.' He grinned. 'I'm deeply indebted to him.'

I sat back in my chair, clasped my hands in front of my face and gave him a long, speculative look. He returned it with a humorous one of his own, then flung his leg down, leaning forward to balance his elbows on his knees. 'It's this place,' he said, with sudden weariness. 'Don't you feel it?' In an almost supplicatory gesture, he reached out to me with his right hand, rotated the hand in the air so that the palm faced upwards, then let it fall again and his head sink between his shoulders.

'Go on,' I said.

He raised his head and let his gaze rest on me for a moment. Then he got to his feet and walked to the window behind me, leaning against the frame, his hands in his pockets, looking out wistfully at the lighted windows opposite.

'What goes on over there?' he asked. I turned my chair so that I too was facing the window.

'Operations.'

'So late?' he murmured. Before I had a chance to explain about the empty operating theatres, the memo and the light from the corridor, he interrupted me. 'This place,' he began again, 'it's not . . .' and he let out the remains of his breath, apparently at a loss for words. A moment later he made a third attempt to explain himself and soon he was speaking feverishly. The muscles in his face twisted and from time to time he squeezed his eyes shut, as if refusing to see. This feeling of his, he said, he wanted to try and put it into words while it was tangible, while he could almost see it in front of him. The hospital was not continuous with the rest of the world, that was the nub of it. What was valuable outside had little or no value in here, and vice versa. It was like a reminder of what was *no longer*, an outmoded currency, kept for nostalgic reasons behind glass at the museum. What was certain was that he felt it most acutely when he had just returned from the front, when he'd seen men and women fighting, giving up their lives for a noble cause . . . that was the opposite, the currency in use . . . He drifted off again, he seemed preoccupied with his own thoughts.

I prompted him gently. 'Can you explain it a little better, this feeling?'

He shook his head. He'd thought about it a great deal while he was away. When he thought about the hospital, the image that most easily sprang to mind was that of a beehive. It had sectors for workers and for drones. Nestor was a worker, down there in his tiny, dark cell; the nurses were workers too, of course; even the doctors, the consultants, though perhaps of a higher caste. The drones, well, clearly they were the patients: the sick who lay in bed, waited on hand and foot, adding nothing to the productivity of the place but fertilising it, keeping it viable. Not alive, not dead, not awake, not sleeping; nevertheless proclaiming their existence and the right to be tended to. Just as in a beehive, light, temperature and ventilation were strictly controlled by some central thermostat. There was a force driving the functioning of the organism, an invisible hand which guided it and which all its inhabitants blindly obeyed. Like any living organism, it had to be fed. The influx of human beings through that great portal was greater than the efflux, at least that's how it seemed to him, a casual observer. You could see a person enter the building and move off to the sector relevant to his age, sex or complaint, which was not the same as your own. You would never see him again. And since you never saw him again, it was easy to form the impression that he never left the hospital, even though you yourself might be through in a morning. He knew Fleur Bartholomew, he was on good terms with her. He always knew at least a couple of the nurses, though of course they came and went. It amused him that they treated him as a newcomer, when he had been visiting that hospital longer than they had worked there, longer than many of them had been qualified. Each time he returned they greeted him warmly, they seemed happy to see him. They never asked where he had been or how he had occupied his time. He used to wonder why, until he realised that their attention was fully taken up by what was going on beneath their noses. The building itself bred intrigue. In this living catacomb, you remained invisible just as long as you abided by the rules. But any individual who strayed beyond his or her colour-coded sector, who tried to impose his own will on others or was simply curious to know what universe he inhabited, became immediately noticeable, like a fox in a hen house. The alarm would be raised and continue to echo long after he had drifted through and emerged into the daylight beyond. His alter ego, Nestor, was a case in point. So was he, to a certain extent.

With that he fell silent. I thought about what he'd said. 'It's an illusion you have, and it comes from these walls.' I rapped my knuckles on the broad windowsill. 'The building is only a century or two old, you see, and it's still sound. The public purse never has anything to spare for us. So we're forced to live by the outdated notions of a Victorian psychiatrist.'

His gaze came to rest on me. 'I admire you,' he said, 'and I want to be fair. The old folks were surprised when I agreed to this experiment, but that's because they don't understand. When the time comes, it will count in my favour. It will strengthen my position. The court will see that I have been open to all propositions, while at the same time protecting my wife from these doctors' worst excesses. It will come down on my side.' He corrected himself: 'On her side.'

'I see you've thought it all through,' I said, drily.

He gave a little half-smile and moved away from the window. 'I think I'd like to go back now,' he said. 'Come if you like.'

We took the lift to the fifth floor. The nurse was back at her post, yawning and flicking through some notes. She was young, with flame-red hair tied back in a frizzy plait. Her eyes widened when she saw Levy, who winked at her. 'It's long past visiting time, but Tina will make an exception for me, won't you, Tina?'

Glancing nervously at me, she started to say something about regulations. I told her it was all right and she batted her eyelashes at Levy. We passed into the corridor and I thought I detected a small rise in temperature. It must have been my imagination because the temperature never changed up there, but it seemed to me very slightly humid, like a greenhouse, and as usual for that time of night, dimly lit. 'Like overgrown larvae,' Levy growled as he loped at my side. 'Babes that clawed their way back into the womb.' I shivered, because the same thought had crossed my mind only an hour or so earlier, but I kept my eyes on the floor. He asked me if I knew their stories, these patients whose rooms we were passing, and I was ashamed to realise I did not. Only the name of Diane's immediate neighbour, Mr Aziz.

'It's a sorry litany,' he said, and summed up each one's life history as we passed the open doorway to his or her room.

'This one's wife of sixty-seven years died, he pined for ten days, had a stroke and slipped into a coma. He won't last long, he's lost the will to live. That's why they've put him here, nearest the exit. That one overdosed, deliberately or not we'll never know. Anyhow he failed and he's only twenty-one. This one, with the latex allergy, she's been in and out of psychiatric institutions all her life. Bulimia, self-mutilation, you name it. She's finally back in the only place she feels safe. And last but not least, Aziz. His story is almost too banal to tell. He came here searching for a better life, of course. He opened a shop. But the climate didn't suit his wife, she died and he was left all alone. One day he stepped into the road to rescue a bird, a fledgling that had fallen out of its nest, and a car knocked him down. He was an old man even then, and lonely. But still they keep him on. They don't know what else to do with him.'

At last we stood on the threshold of Diane's room. 'And here is the senior resident, the foundation block of the hospital, the justification for its existence and the greatest enigma of them all. My queen bee . . .'

He moved forward until he was standing by the side of the bed, and clasped his brown, sinewy hands behind his back, so that I could see the black hairs that emerged from his sleeves and grew halfway down from the wrists to the knuckles. There he stood very still for a moment or two, as if paying his respects at a coffin. I came up beside him just in time to see her joyful smile fade. 'She's pleased to see me, as always,' he muttered. 'She's a most conscientious hostess.'

He bent to kiss her perfunctorily on the forehead, then

crossed the room to the papered wall. From the angle of his head I guessed it was the picture of the artist in her studio that had caught his attention, that picture that drew every eye, of the patient as she once was. He raised a hand as if about to pluck it from the collage, hesitated, made a fist of the hand and shoved it back into his trouser pocket. A moment later he turned back, very pale, and sank down into the rocking chair. 'That little statue,' he whispered, resting his head against the back of it, 'I gave it to her.'

I lowered myself on to the wooden chair so that now I was facing him across the bed. He kept his gaze fixed on the ceiling. For a moment he seemed to have trouble breathing. He cleared his throat without shifting his gaze and told me that the statuette was a souvenir of their honeymoon. He had taken her to Florence, at her mother's suggestion, to see David. They queued for several hours. At one point, losing patience, he suggested they give it up and go back to the hotel, but Diane refused to leave. They shuffled forward in their turn, her tranquil gaze directed over the heads of those in front of them, like pilgrims visiting a shrine. When at last they reached their destination, he stood a little way back while his bride walked right up to the pedestal. She was standing in front of the statue, admiring it, when a lunatic broke past the monitors, shoved her aside and, wielding a hammer, smashed David's big toe.

He lifted his head to look at me. It was all over the papers, he said. Surely I remembered the scandal? Yes, I replied. He nodded, fell silent. Diane was extremely affected by it, he recalled. She had wanted to see the statue for so long and finally she had. She had caught a brief glimpse of perfection before it was shattered for ever in front of her eyes. But that wasn't what upset her most. What upset her was that in the moment before the madman rushed up, she had had a similar impulse herself. Yes, the thought had actually crossed her mind to do David some damage. She understood that madman, she sympathised with him. Levy had laughed at her, because she was such a sweet, affectionate girl. There wasn't an ounce of violence in her. 'My wife,' he murmured, letting his eyelids fall, 'my wife . . .'

Leaning forward in his chair, he laid his arms on the counterpane and his head on his arms. His torso shook with great sobs. The movement dislodged Diane's head, so that it rolled towards me on the pillow. A line of spittle ran down her chin from the corner of her mouth, her gaze glided past me and on her lips was a sardonic smile.

13

A month had passed since, beneath the intense gaze of Mezzanotte, I had initiated our patient into the workings of the Mind-Reading Device, and I had yet to see a response. I wasn't disheartened. I knew from my own experience the mental effort required to manipulate the device, I knew how hard it could be even for a healthy human being, so I was prepared to wait. As the days and weeks passed, however, I found myself thinking about her more and more. Her face with its alternating expressions of joy and irony began to insinuate itself into my dreams. The idea had already occurred to me, and now took root in my mind as strongly as if she had said it to me herself, that my pupil was bored. I decided to give Nestor the task of making the exercises more entertaining for her. Mezzanotte gave me his blessing, and one morning I headed down to the basement. Nestor sat hunched over his little card table, the habitual roll-up tucked behind his right ear. He cringed as I announced myself and without turning round, muttered, 'I'm busy.'

I walked up to him anyway and he raised his head to

reveal a swollen and split lower lip. 'What's it to you?' he replied, when I asked if he'd been in a fight. He flicked disconsolately through a few pages of the magazine he had been reading.

I explained why I had come. I wanted him to make some adjustments to the system, but in such a way that it continued to exploit any skills Diane might have already acquired – mental acrobatics she may well have been practising, but whose electrical output wasn't yet robust enough to produce a trace on our screens.

Nestor glanced up thoughtfully at the little wooden cross. Pushing his chair back, he got to his feet and paced the room. He stroked his chin, came to a standstill and pointed his nail-bitten, tarry forefinger at me.

'We replace the wave with a Pac-Man,' he said. 'It just means tinkering with the cursor a bit. The Pac-Man marks the signal at the present time, rather than the changing signal over time. She has to send it towards the fruit, which it gobbles up – just like in kids' games.'

I nodded, pleased. 'What else?'

He paced up and down a bit more, mumbling to himself, and came to a halt again. He could invent a points system, he said, and a gong or a musical note for each bullseye. Yes, yes, I replied, that was just the thing. He smiled as far as his split lip would allow him and I saw that he had also lost a tooth. Could he have it ready by the end of the week? I asked. He sucked in his breath in a kind of inverted whistle that seemed to indicate I was asking a lot. He'd see what he could do. I left him hunched over his desk again, a pair of mammoth headphones covering his ears, fiddling with the switches and dials on the boxes that were arranged around his table.

Looking back on the events of the following ten days, I had the feeling that I had somehow brought them upon myself, that by tampering with the Mind-Reading Device I had knocked our fragile routine out of kilter. The first sign that something was wrong was that Denise failed to turn up for her visit the next day, at least she had not appeared by the time I left Diane's room. That evening I read in the paper that a question had been raised in Parliament about the crumbling state of our oldest and most highly regarded hospitals. Ours was held up as an example. While money was frittered away on peacekeeping operations in faraway countries, it sank into a state of decrepitude. Shouldn't our hospitals be the gleaming beacons of our civilisation, the politician who raised the question asked; the health of the nation our foremost concern? Somewhere along the way our values had been turned upside down, he said, and it was a disgrace. The question triggered a heated debate, and the newspapers devoted their front pages to the story. It seemed that people were fed up with the war, and the hospital question provided them with a scapegoat through which to vent their frustration.

It didn't occur to me that the two things, Denise's absence and the question in Parliament, might be connected until I saw John Wraith the following morning. When I asked him why his wife had not turned up as usual, he went very pale and rubbed his forehead. He was worried, he said. Denise had been pulling strings with her powerful friends; he knew that she had been planning something and now he had discovered what it was. What the consequences would be, he had no idea, but he was afraid that his daughter would be swept up in something that could be harmful to her, and that he wouldn't be able to protect her from it.

I gave Diane her lesson as usual, packed up the equipment and waited to see if Denise would appear. I was standing at the window, looking down into the garden and thinking what a haven of peace it seemed in contrast to the angry turmoil of the world outside, when I heard her voice behind me. I spun round, only to find her blinking out at me from the television screen. Behind her rose the familiar redbrick façade of the hospital, and she was holding a photograph up to the camera – the picture of a smiling Diane holding a paint-smeared palette. I quickly switched the machine off and ran out of the room towards the nurse's station where I knew there was a small TV set. I saw most of the interview there. A tearful Denise spoke about the beautiful young woman in the photograph, her daughter, who had been cut down in her prime; who might have recovered some semblance of a normal existence, even pursued her dream of becoming an artist, if the doctors had not been hampered by their outdated equipment and lack of funds. She had kept quiet for a decade, but now that the courts were threatening to switch off her daughter's life support, simply to free up a bed, she had decided to speak out.

The next morning the papers reported that Denise's plea had provoked an outcry. Women's organisations and disabled rights groups had rallied to her cause, as had the religious right. Levy was attacked in the pages of his own newspaper.

John Wraith turned up at the usual time, massaged the patient's twisted hands and left as soon as I appeared. He seemed preoccupied. Denise arrived a few minutes before the end of the lesson. Her cheeks were flushed and she asked me if I had seen her on TV. She didn't wait for a reply, but kissed her daughter on the forehead and whispered to her, warmly, 'You'll see, darling, things will happen now.'

That morning, Fleur Bartholomew and I were due to have one of our fortnightly meetings to discuss Patient DL, but when I arrived at her office I found it empty. I returned to my own office on the second floor to find a message from Nestor: he had made the modifications we had discussed, and the new version of the device was ready to be put through its paces. I tested it the following day, Friday, with no response. I told myself that Diane needed time to adjust to the changes and I left for the weekend, thinking that by Monday all the trouble would have blown over.

I was wrong. By Monday, not only had workers walked out of ours and many other hospitals in the city, but workers from other sectors had gone on strike in support of them. I walked the short distance from my flat to the hospital. The streets were almost deserted, the construction sites abandoned and the cranes on the skyline still and silent. The weekend rubbish had not been collected and spilled out into the gutter from overfilled sacks that had been ransacked by dogs or foxes in the night. A police car crawled past me, while a tramp trailing shoelaces and a grubby sleeping bag stared hungrily through the bars of a grille that covered a darkened supermarket window. My own footsteps rang out, echoing, as I passed through one of the low tunnels into the square. The hospital loomed into view, a comforting sight until I spotted the small band of women gathered in front of it, who were waving placards and chanting.

There was no way to avoid passing quite close to this group and as I did so a woman's arm shot out and grasped my own, forcing me to stop and face her. 'There are plenty of reasons to be concerned about what's going on behind those doors,' she said, conspiratorially, and jerked her head towards the hospital entrance. Two security guards stood either side of it, I noticed. Jerking my arm away from her, I slipped through the crowd and discreetly flashed one of the guards my pass. As soon as I was inside I headed for Fleur's room, but there was no sign of her. For the rest of that day I went about my work with a growing sense of unease. I timed my visit to Diane so as not to cross paths with John Wraith, and I packed up early so as to avoid Denise. I switched off the television as soon as I walked into the room, and did not switch it back on again on my way out. The next morning I went straight to Fleur's office, and to my relief, this time she was there. She had just returned from her early rounds and she was wearing a white coat over her ankle-length, rose-coloured robe. The rose of her turban made a striking contrast with the white of her clinician's uniform, but she looked tired and drawn. I asked her what was going on.

'Sit down,' she said, without a trace of a smile. With some trepidation I lowered myself into one of the plaid-upholstered armchairs. As far as she was concerned, Fleur said irritably, nothing was wrong with the hospitals that hadn't always been wrong with them. However, recent events had conspired to paint a bad picture of this particular establishment. There had been a fresh outbreak of the superbug – this time in the neonatal unit, where it had caused two deaths. Sometime in the last week undercover reporters had infiltrated the building and unearthed the defunct computer system in the basement. There had been demands for an inquiry, and it was when the minister concerned refused on the grounds that systems of accountability were already in place that the strike was called. Large numbers of workers had walked out. As if by unspoken consent, or perhaps a feeling of loyalty to the beleaguered institution, the majority of the staff employed in this hospital had continued to turn up for work. But a small group had broken ranks, leaving it more short-staffed than usual. The fact that the hospital was still functioning drew the nation's attention. Thanks to Denise's appearance before the cameras people now associated that building with the beautiful girl who, for ten years, had lain paralysed in a room on the fifth floor, a victim of government cuts. To top it all, Levy had written an ill-timed and, in Fleur's view, ill-judged response to his critics, in which he defiantly defended his family's right to privacy. That article had been published in the weekend newspapers, and the upshot of it all was that Diane Levy had become the focal point of the unrest. She had been forgotten for a decade, the country had gone about its business without her, but suddenly her picture was plastered all over the papers and her name tripped as easily off people's tongues as that of any movie star. She had become the figurehead of a movement. The face of courage, they were calling her.

Fleur fell silent. I frowned. 'Has word of the experiment got out?' I asked her.

'No,' she sighed. 'The hospital has managed to guard at least one of its secrets.'

Without warning, she closed her eyes and covered her face with her hands. It was only then that I realised she was exhausted. I sprang up and led her to a chair. When I pressed my palm to her forehead, it was warm. I told her she should take a day off and rest, or she would become ill herself, and I pointed to the photographs of her children on the wall. 'If you get sick, who will look after them?' When she saw that I was indicating the photos, she raised a puzzled face to mine. 'But those pictures are old, Sarah. My children are all grown up now.'

We stared at each other and I realised that Fleur, too, had grown older. Not suddenly, or dramatically, nevertheless without my noticing she had aged. There was some puckering of the skin around her mouth and the tight coils of hair at her temples had turned to silver. I resumed my seat and for what seemed like a long time we sat in silence, not quite meeting one another's eye. Rain began beating loudly against the window, I glanced up at it. Fleur turned towards it at the same time, and as we turned away again our eyes met. 'What is it?' I asked, afraid. 'Has something else happened?'

There was a long pause before, with some reluctance, she announced that Mezzanotte had been summoned to appear before a committee of inquiry. The blame for the whole scandal had fallen on the university, since the hospital came under its authority, and those at the top had set up a tribunal to look into it. She wouldn't say any more, but with a frightened glance at the door, she added that it might strengthen the professor's defence if I had some encouraging data to show from the mind-reading project.

'But I haven't anything,' I told her, raising my palms to the ceiling in a helpless gesture. 'I need more time.'

She looked at me wearily. 'You still think it's just a question of time?'

'Yes,' I said, firmly. And then I told her what I really thought. I described my first meeting with John Wraith, when he had appeared to communicate telepathically with his daughter. I told her about the tears that had flooded down Diane's cheeks during the TV programme about David – and the story of the statue as I later heard it from her husband. I listed the countless other tiny reactions I had witnessed, that on their own meant nothing, but combined, seemed to indicate an elusive but quick intelligence. And I tried to put into words a feeling that had been growing in me and that I had so far failed to articulate, even to myself. 'Every now and then,' I said, 'I have the feeling that she's conducting the whole performance.'

I stopped, afraid of annoying Fleur. But in quite a mild tone, as if she were genuinely interested, she asked me how I found the patient's relatives. Encouraged, I thought for a moment. I had noticed, I said, that the behaviour of all three of them was quite eccentric in relation to Diane, which was hardly surprising considering the emotional strain they were under. The last few months had been particularly hard on them, since Levy had decided to seek a court injunction to bring her life to a close, thereby giving their anxiety a focus in time. What was perhaps harder to understand was that their ideas about her, or rather what was left of her, had evolved in such different directions. Each one was now isolated and unable to comfort the other two, which was sad to see.

'And yet,' she said, thoughtfully, 'they still have one thing in common.'

I looked at her and she went on. According to her, each one of them saw an ally in Diane. They read sympathy into her silence. They confided in her. They thought she understood and they drew strength from her. When they left her room and went out into the world, they felt her presence at their side. All this despite the absence of any sign, and even though they could see for themselves how damaged she was. It was an illusion, she said, and whatever happened I must not fall for it.

Before I could reply, there was a knock at the door. 'Ah,' she said, without getting up. 'Here is a gentleman who, if I'm not very much mistaken, brings you glad tidings.'

A balding, middle-aged man wearing a blazer with shiny brass buttons and a pair of thick, round glasses entered the room. He was small, humped and muscular as a muntjak, and across his bald pate stretched a few wispy strands of grey hair. There was something of the circus about him, or the travelling salesman. I stood as he entered, and found when he came up close to me that I was a good head taller than him. He peered up at me through his spectacles. His myopic eyes were magnified by the thick lenses. A vein throbbed at his temple.

Fleur introduced us from her armchair with a wave of her long arm, and explained my role as coordinator of Mezzanotte's project. In very precise tones, without taking his eyes off me, Professor Harding then apologised for what might seem like his odd manner, but he had to be on his guard.

'Your guard?' I repeated, puzzled. Before he obliged me with an explanation he settled himself in the chair I had occupied until a few moments earlier and energetically crossed his short legs. He was the victim of harassment, he informed me in the same precise, nasal tones; a target for certain extremist groups. These agitators were the right-to-live brigade, but also their counterparts at the other end of the moral spectrum, those who fought for the citizen's right to die. He got them mixed up, they used the same language. According to the first lot, he was a murderer because he sometimes decided that it was in a patient's interest to die. That was straightforward enough, one could follow the logic there. But sometimes he decided that a patient deserved to live. In that case, it was the right-to-die who trailed him morning, noon and night, making his life a misery, wearing him down, and they were altogether more cunning. By depriving a person of the right to end his or her own life, they argued, he was robbing them of their personhood, which made him, once again, a murderer. Whichever way you looked at it, he was evil, a monster. They were outside now, waiting for him to show his face so that they could hurl more abuse at him. He refused to give in to them, and that's why he had walked 'halfway across the city' to get here today; why he had 'fought his way through the hostile hordes' to see his patient. Behind his thick lenses he fluttered his eyelashes which, due to the magnifying effect, appeared rather long and feminine. He pouted and re-crossed his legs. Then he addressed Fleur, who listened sleepily, supporting her head with its rose-coloured turban on the palm of her hand. I perched on her desk, curious to hear what he had to say.

'I have now completed my investigations,' he began, portentously.

He had carried out a whole battery of tests on the patient, he said, but the one that had convinced him was the simplest. He asked her to close her eyes, and she did. He asked her to open them again, and she did that too. He gave her a whole series of verbal commands, and she obeyed them all, to the letter. Finally he thumped her between the eyebrows, as hard as he could, and she opened and closed her eyes several times in rapid succession.

Fleur and I exchanged glances. He went on, oblivious. It was his view that Diane Levy was cortically and cognitively intact, a prisoner in her own paralysed body. She was, he had established, a classic case of locked-in syndrome, the condition he had defined and on the elucidation of which he had made his name. She was buried alive, incarcerated in a glass coffin, fully equipped with all her senses and thus condemned to gaze out at the world until some kind soul put an end to her suffering. Able to see, hear, smell, taste, but unable to act. A receptacle filled to the brim with sensory information, with no motor output, no safety valve, no means of expression – except for that tiny exception, her ability to blink, which was so feeble as to be more accurately described as a leak rather than a channel of information.

He fell silent, and looked from one to the other of us.

'You thumped her?' I said.

Yes, he replied blithely, and she had opened and closed her eyes several times rapidly, which probably meant that she was able to feel pain. After a pause, during which Fleur noisily cleared her throat, I asked him if someone else had witnessed this examination, or if he had filmed it.

'No one saw it but me,' he replied, almost proudly. I asked him how he explained the fact that in the previous ten years, she had made no sign.

'Tut-tut!' he said, raising a warning finger. 'Now you're asking me to speculate!'

He continued to look from one to the other of us expectantly.

In the end, Fleur thanked him. 'As soon as I receive your report,' she said, 'I will add it to the others.'

That seemed to satisfy him, and he jumped up and shook hands. Opening the door by just a narrow gap, he stuck his head out. Apparently reassured that the coast was clear, he squeezed himself out backwards before pulling the door shut behind him, like someone trying not to let a cat out.

I glanced at Fleur. She returned my look with a dull one of her own. Since Denise had made her plea to the nation, she said, there had been renewed interest in Diane from the medical community. There would be another expert the following week, one the week after that and so on until she had been examined, palpated and pummelled by all the experts in the land. That is if the courts didn't find in favour of Levy, in which case there would be no more experts, because no more patient. And of course, no more experiment either. She delivered all this in a gloomy monotone, without any of her usual good humour. Then she spelled it out for me: time was running out for Diane. As she rose from her chair, a little unsteadily, I gathered that I, too, was dismissed.

When I returned to my office, there was a note on my desk: Mezzanotte wanted me to meet him that afternoon at five o'clock. I puzzled over the note for a minute or two, because the place I was summoned to was not the new institute of which he was director, but a numbered room in the main university building. Probably he had some new piece of equipment he wanted to show me, I thought, and put it out of my mind. I worked hard all afternoon and left just before five. It was getting dark as I stepped through the grand portal, and in the west, over the rooftops, the sun was setting in a blaze of colour. I circled the little band of women, who were now gathered round a small brazier that lit up their faces, warming their hands and murmuring in low voices as if they were the last human beings on earth. The streets beyond the square were empty and glistening after the rain. I passed an ordinary-looking terraced house with a plaque announcing that the first anaesthetic had been delivered there, then the university library – one of the oldest and largest in the world – and the debating union where some of our finest politicians had cut their teeth. I felt a great sigh rise up in me and I let it out into the rain-scented air. Once I had been proud of those monuments, those symbols of the greatness of my adopted nation; now they appeared to me like relics of a bygone age. The city itself seemed frozen in time, petrified, brought to its knees by a slip of a girl who couldn't lift her little finger, let alone issue a command.

Passing through a pair of giant wrought-iron gates, I crossed the marble, colonnaded space in front of the university and gazed up at the lighted windows of the rector's rooms on the first floor. I quickened my step and soon I was running up the wide central staircase, two at a time. I turned in the direction of the Department of Anatomy, situated towards the back of the building, and passed the door to the classroom in which I had once interviewed my insomniacs. I walked the length of a windowless passage and climbed a staircase into what seemed like an attic, because the ceiling and the door frames were much lower than on the floor below – so low that a man of the professor's height would have to stoop to enter. Thinking I must have taken a wrong turn, I began to retrace my steps. Just then I saw a door marked with only a number, 212, and no name. Checking the professor's note, I saw that this was the place to which I had been summoned, and knocked.

As the door swung back, I peered into a narrow space which stretched back to an even narrower window beyond which all that was visible, and audible, was a cluster of roaring ventilation shafts thrusting up into the darkening sky. The room wasn't much bigger than a cupboard. Right at the back of it, a desk that had been wedged into its tiny width was overhung on both sides by shelves bulging with books and journals. Behind the desk, silhouetted against the window, sat a familiar figure. I couldn't see his face very well. There was a standard lamp with a yellow shade behind me, near the door, and a lamp on the desk, but otherwise no source of light in the room besides the window.

As my eyes adapted to the gloom, I saw that Mezzanotte was sitting back in his chair, very still. Thinking perhaps he was ill, I crossed the room quickly and peered down at him. I could see that he had turned his head to look back at me, but at first I couldn't make out his expression. His eyes had receded into their sockets, his cheeks were gaunt and the lines on his forehead and around his mouth seemed to have deepened still further. I registered these changes vaguely, because there was something more disturbing still about his appearance. His shirt collar was unbuttoned and open wide, exposing the white, fleshless folds of his neck. Without the ivory silk cravat that I had always known him wear, he appeared indecently exposed.

I asked him what he was doing there. Without moving his head, he raised an eyebrow.

'What, you don't like my new quarters?'

I scanned his face, as if the truth might somehow be revealed there, but he simply returned my interrogative gaze with an amused one of his own. I glanced at the creaking ventilation shafts behind him, and perhaps he guessed the direction of my thoughts because he explained, in the same laconic tone, that his new situation was temporary. In the wake of the recent controversy concerning the hospital, he had been relieved of the directorship of the institute and had given up his office to the new incumbent. The physical upheaval was naturally very inconvenient, but as soon as the current misunderstanding was sorted out, he had been assured he would be moving again, to new and larger premises.

At that moment I understood that he was being punished, though for what and by whom I didn't immediately grasp. Hot waves of indignation pulsed through me and I demanded to know who was behind it. He laughed softly. He had published fewer papers than his underlings in the last year, he said, in order to devote his time to the mind-reading project, and in so doing had drawn the hawklike scrutiny of the university auditors. They had now made their displeasure known. He gestured with his head to indicate the room.

Slowly I shook my head. 'They have such short memories?'

The professor smiled. 'In this place, one continually has to prove one's worth. Which is just as it should be, of course.'

His smile faded and when he spoke again it was with a hint of bitterness. I must be aware, he said, that to take a risk was no longer acceptable in this university. These days, the only questions it was permissible to ask were those to which one already knew the answer. People wanted results and they wanted them quickly. The university would suffer, but that was in the future, possibly long after his own death. Removing a handkerchief from his pocket, he dabbed at his neck (it was warm in the small room).

I stared at him, and felt a lump rise to my throat. People had always been suspicious of him. He saw further than the university, further than the city, and he refused to concern himself with their minutiae. For that they couldn't forgive him, so they condemned him to a poky cupboard with a view of rusting pipes. They hauled him up in front of a tribunal and tried to bring him low with trumped-up charges. I opened my mouth to speak, to express my outrage, but he interrupted me. He asked me quickly if I had any progress to report. I hesitated. I couldn't bear to bring him more bad news. But what would be the use of lying? I lowered my eyes.

It was then that he told me the reason he had summoned me there that afternoon. He had enrolled two new subjects in the experiment, he said, long-term patients at a hospital just outside the city. 'One is in the later stages of motor neurone disease, the other has suffered a brain haemorrhage. Both are incapacitated, quite incapable of independent movement. One, the woman, is progressing in leaps and bounds. She's already on to the alphabet. Mentally she is remarkably agile. The man is doing well too, though he tires quickly. I'm confident they'll both have the hang of it before long.'

I stared at him in dismay. 'But what about Diane?'

He stiffened, spoke sharply. He still had the highest hopes for Patient DL, he said, but her case was complicated. Her scans were too ambiguous for his liking. The family was at loggerheads. He couldn't afford to waste any more time on unproductive subjects, though I, of course, could do as I wished. For himself, he had already risked too much with this project and now it had to bear fruit. His new candidates were either alone in the world, or their relatives were not interfering. Both were free of psychiatric complications. In fact, they were ideal for his purposes. He expected to see concrete results within a matter of weeks.

As if the effort of making this little speech had exhausted him, he sank back in his chair. 'Now if you don't mind,' he murmured, 'I have work to do.' I gazed down at him, then turned and left the room.

14

It happened at 10.17 on a Monday morning in early March. I know because I noted it in my logbook. Six weeks into the experiment, at 10.17 precisely, I saw a blip in the cursor's trajectory. My heart skipped a beat, I blinked at the screen, held my breath and waited. There was nothing more. Perhaps her efforts had exhausted her. I prayed that Denise would miraculously miss her appointment, so that I could extend the lesson, but she turned up a few minutes early as usual. I rushed to put the equipment away and left her to her strange ritual. I skulked about the entrance hall, watching the lift doors and waiting for her to appear. Nestor came up for a smoke, looked at me curiously and descended again without a word. A trio of nurses saw me and whispered behind their hands. I took no notice of them. I must have looked a sight, pacing up and down, gnawing at my cuticles, talking to myself, gazing up, trance-like, at the patches of sky revealed through the glass panes in the ceiling, while porters steered their wheelchairs around me. If only they had seen what I had seen, perhaps they would sympathise. At last I had evidence, if only of the flimsiest kind, that my patient was conscious; more than that, that she was able to hear, attend and perform a difficult task. She was in there, clamouring to get out. Now I was forced to wait, bide my time, while her mother rubbed glutinous ointment into her arms and regaled her with trivia. When the lift doors parted to reveal Denise, the disgorged basket now balanced lightly over her arm, I stepped behind the signpost. She paused on the threshold, framed by the great portal, a muffled cheer went up from her loyal band of supporters outside and she gave a little wave. Then she was gone and I flew back up to the fifth floor.

Once there, I assembled the equipment as quickly as I could. There it was again, the Pac-Man making a lunge for the cartoon apple. 'The old man was right!' I whispered, hardly able to contain my excitement. I waited another half-hour but there was nothing more. I told myself it could have been an artefact, but when I returned in the late afternoon there was no mistaking it. Once again, Diane sent the Pac-Man hurtling towards its target, which it struck with deadly accuracy, like a viper and at the speed of lightning. Since Nestor had arranged that a bullseye now produced a drum roll, the sound broke over me like distant thunder, or the grumbling of a disgruntled god.

I hardly trusted my own ears or eyes – even after the second repetition – so I hurried down to Nestor for corroboration. There was no reply to my knock and when I tried the door it was locked. That meant that although the responses had certainly been recorded, and an electronic log of them now existed, they had not passed before his eyes on their way into the computer's memory banks. That in turn meant that I was the only person to know of their existence, besides the patient herself. As I strolled back along the basement corridor and up the concrete steps, an idea began to take shape in my head.

In ten years, I said to myself, she hasn't made a sign to her relatives, the hospital staff or any of the so-called experts who have passed through her room – except for Harding, whose claims we can safely ignore since there were no witnesses and his methods are, to say the least, unconventional. She hasn't used the direction of her gaze, the control of which we strongly suspect she retains, to let them know she can hear their every word. Could it be that she would rather they thought her deaf, dumb, beyond comprehension?

On the other hand, she had chosen to communicate with me. Careful examination of the facts led me to conclude that she would rather I kept that to myself, until such time as she could make her wishes clear. I would therefore keep the breakthrough a secret, until the day when Diane progressed to a more advanced handling of the device and could speak in sentences, or until a court decision to withdraw her feeding tube looked imminent, whichever happened first. I wouldn't even tell Mezzanotte, who had already abandoned her and found consolation in his other students – unless, of course, his own future hung in the balance, in which case I would think again.

That was how my reasoning went. By the time I reached my office I had examined my decision from all angles and found nothing wrong with it. On the contrary, it seemed to me the only rational way forward. Nevertheless, a nagging doubt remained at the back of my mind, not so much a doubt even, as the burden of having to keep such a weighty decision to myself. So once I had cleared the last file from my desk, and dealt with the last correspondence, I wandered down to the geriatric wing, which seemed strangely quiet, and on into the little chapel.

I found the vicar in the vestry, ironing his surplice. He didn't seem surprised to see me, but led me in silence to the front pew of one of the six sectors, where we sat down close to one another. 'A friend of mine,' I began, and paused, 'a patient, that is, came to me today with a dilemma. He asked for my advice.'

I heard myself speaking the way people do in films, and inwardly I laughed. I was enjoying myself, though the vicar, who must have been ten years my junior, in his late twenties perhaps, listened earnestly.

I told him the story, lightly disguised. A woman had gone missing. The search for her had gone on for many years. Her family, accepting at last that she was dead, were devastated by their loss. One day, out of the blue, the woman came back and presented herself to this patient of mine. She asked him not to tell anyone else she was alive.

The vicar bowed his head over his clasped hands. I finished up with the following question: '. . . and so, since this woman has been missing for a decade, and many people have been searching for her, is it wrong for my friend, my patient rather, to keep her whereabouts a secret?'

The vicar raised his head and gazed at me with clear blue eyes. I could see that he already had his answer prepared, the situation was clear-cut to him, and that annoyed me. So as he opened his mouth to speak, I interrupted him. 'Excuse me, Vicar, but I haven't been quite truthful with you. It's not a patient of mine, it's me. And the woman isn't missing, she's lying upstairs in the north wing, in a state of consciousness verging on coma. Perhaps you've heard about her, she's the one in the newspapers. I only told you the story the way I did because I thought it would be easier for you to understand. I assumed you wouldn't have come across anything quite like it before. But I see I was wrong to do that. You see, the real situation differs in certain important respects. Some people would like to turn off this woman's life support. She wouldn't suffer. If they deprived her of insulin for a day or two death would be painless for her. Today, though, she spoke to me. It's the first sign of life she's given in a decade, though she could have made herself known earlier. She had the means at her disposal, yet she chose to keep quiet. And I ask myself, why? Why should she choose to speak now, and why to me? I'm afraid that she has something against her family, that if I tell them about this new development, which officially, of course, I'm obliged to do, I will scare her away. She'll lapse into a permanent silence, possibly even coma, and soon death.'

The vicar looked frightened. 'What did she say to you?'

I told him that she didn't say anything, as such, and I explained how the Mind-Reading Device worked. His eyes opened wider as I spoke: he'd never have thought such a thing was possible. 'Of course I know that ward, I've been there once or twice, patients have asked for me . . .'

I looked at him. I was surprised to hear that, I said, because

I had been led to believe that no one ever died on that ward. He went very pale. He sprang up and I stood too. He was trembling all over. He told me to follow my heart. God and my conscience would be my guide. Then he laid his hand hastily on my shoulder and hurried back into the vestry. I watched him go. I felt sorry for him, but it wasn't my fault. I had really hoped that he could help me and now that he had gone, I felt terribly alone. Nervous laughter bubbled up inside me, I tried to suppress it but it escaped anyway and ran round the walls of the little chapel and up to the vaulted ceiling. The door to the vestry was closed, but even so the vicar must have heard it.

15

To my great disappointment Diane gave me no further sign. Weeks passed. The strike was called off, a deal was struck, new hospitals were promised. Levy continued to push his petition through the courts, the women remained camped out in the square and the controversy over Diane staggered on in the pages of the newspapers, claiming fewer and fewer column inches until at last the journalists lost interest entirely. During that time the TV in her room broadcast the occasional bulletin about her. I no longer bothered to turn it off when it happened, thinking that the mention of her own name by an unfamiliar voice might just rouse her from her torpor. Day after day, listlessly, I stood at the window and let the sound wash over me. Levy had vanished again, but Mr and Mrs Wraith kept up their daily visits according to the usual pattern.

One day I was gazing down into the hospital garden and I saw that the flower beds were filled with daffodils, some with their buds closed, ready to burst, others already unfurled and lapping up the feeble sunshine. Green buds covered the cherry and almond trees. Winter had receded like a tide and spring was advancing in its wake. Behind me, the television reported a hiatus in the hostilities. Our troops were pulling out of the eastern sector.

The following Saturday I went for a walk on the embankment. There was a chill in the air but people were out in the gardens that ran alongside the river, delighting in the snowdrops and the croci that pushed their way up through the damp, mossy ground. On the stone rampart overlooking the water a tramp laid out his lunch: two oysters, a half lemon and a bottle of cider, two-thirds drunk. He brought an oyster knife out of his knapsack and danced a little jig, a breeze ruffling his hair, a soiled sleeping bag curled around his shoulders like some grotesque and bloody stole.

I walked on and saw ahead of me, sitting on a bench with a newspaper folded in his lap, a slender, satyr-like man with a bronzed, bearded face. He sat very still, apparently entranced by the little waves that caressed a muddy piece of shore visible at that point through a gap in the wall. It was Levy. He raised his head as I stopped in front of him. 'Hello,' he said, smiling as if he had been expecting me. I sat down and he reached out and stroked my cheek. I blinked in surprise, he reached out again, more determinedly this time, and I recoiled. He tried once more and I recoiled still further, until my back was arched against the wooden arm of the bench. He let his hand drop.

'Don't you like men?' he asked curiously, and when I didn't reply, 'When did you last make love?' I remained coldly silent until he exploded with, 'Ach, what's the use!' and flung himself back against the bench. Crossing his arms over his chest, he stared moodily out at the river again. I thought of getting up, walking away and so showing my disapproval, but I hesitated a moment too long. Turning back to me, smiling again as if that disconcerting incident had never happened, he asked me politely if I would permit him to tell me a story.

I looked at him. His mood seemed to have swung to the opposite pole and I suspected some trick. But I was also aware that the success or failure of our experiment lay in this creature's hand, that he could withdraw his consent at any moment and that if I annoyed him, I might never see my patient again. 'By all means,' I said, and picking up the newspaper, he began to recount the strange tale of Peter Kastas.

Kastas was a journalist in a country which, at the time of this story, now a few years old, had only recently been freed from a tyrannical dictatorship. Night after night he insinuated himself into locked offices where he systematically photocopied the files of the secret police. His goal was to collect evidence for the tortures, interrogations and murders committed by the military during their fifteen years of power. Among the papers he found were letters that had been confiscated before they reached their destinations. They were written by, or addressed to, names that had since found their way on to lists of 'missing persons'. Some were love letters. They had lipstick kisses on them, or were written on perfumed paper whose scent still lingered.

Kastas didn't want to return these letters to their files; to do so seemed to him yet another violation of the government's victims. Neither could he bring himself to destroy them. What should he do? He wrestled with the dilemma until he hit on a solution. Folding them back into their envelopes, he stuck on new stamps and dropped them into the postbox on his way home each night.

In some cases the letters never arrived: the addresses no longer existed, or there was no one of that name to receive them. Sometimes they brought joy into a household that had been in mourning for years. In other homes, they came as an unwelcome surprise. Perhaps the most shocking case in the latter category was that of a woman with a violent husband and three children, who learned that her childhood sweetheart had not betrayed her, as she had long ago convinced herself, but had been captured and tortured to death. She became morose, depressed. One day her husband slapped her affectionately on the backside and she seized a kitchen knife and stabbed him in the belly. She spilled his guts over the kitchen floor. Kastas, of course, knew nothing about it. Night after night, he carried on posting those fifteen-year-old letters, safe in the knowledge that he was righting a terrible wrong.

Levy lowered the paper and turned to me. 'You're like Kastas,' he said. 'You're his twin.' I had been listening to the story with growing interest, and in a flash I understood why Levy had read it to me. I flushed angrily. I opened my mouth and closed it again, but what could I say? He was watching me, clearly enjoying the effects of his words. His eyes shone, his lips were moist and two feverish spots burned in his cheeks. I forced a smile and stood up, really intending to leave this time. At that point, laughing, he laid a hand on my arm. 'Don't go,' he said. 'It's not often I have intelligent company these days.'

I hesitated and sat down again. Smirking, he set about refolding his newspaper and I turned to watch a small boy wander down the path towards us. He can't have been more than three or four. He was dressed in a pair of dungarees, and every now and then he would squat by a clump of daffodils at the edge of the path, insert his saliva-coated finger into the cup and draw it out, coated with pollen. Gradually he came closer until, holding out the loaded, glistening finger, he stumbled up to Levy. Levy took the finger in his mouth, sucking off the yellow powder with a smack of his lips and a loud 'Delicious!' that made the little boy giggle.

I stared at the child, who was dark with large green eyes, until Levy introduced us. 'Conrad, say hello to Dr Newman. Dr Newman, meet my son.'

The boy gazed at me, then wandered off to fetch more pollen. Levy leaned towards me, and with his eyes downcast, began to speak quietly. I might as well know, he said, that he and the boy's mother were no longer together. They had known each other for a year. It didn't matter who she was. What mattered was that he and Conrad were happy, they didn't need anyone else, which was not to say that he didn't sometimes crave female company, nor that he had stopped loving his wife. Diane was, in fact, the only woman he had ever loved, and he still thought about her all the time. He had met her here, at just this point on the riverbank. When he needed to think about a story he was working on, he would step out of the newspaper's offices, which were just a few streets away, and come here. She would be strolling or sitting on a bench, doing nothing in particular. She was beautiful, of course. Once he had struck up a conversation with her, he found that she was also a good listener. After that they met there every day. He fell in love and lay awake at night dreaming, as one does in that condition, of all the projects they would embark on together, all the adventures they would share and look back on in old age. With her by his side, he would conquer the world.

He looked up at the sky and laughed. 'I understood those crazy architects at last!'

But Diane wasn't like him, he went on. When he talked to her about his grand schemes, his plans for the future, she just smiled and looked away, and if he asked her, impatiently, 'Well, what do you think?' she would reply, 'I don't know. Aren't we happy as we are?' He believed he could bring her round. Looking back, however, he could honestly say that until the day of her accident nothing had ever really moved or inspired her, nothing except David. Perhaps she had fallen in love with the statue. It wasn't impossible. That visit of theirs to Florence certainly had the most energising effect on her. She took up painting. As a surprise, he made the upper floor of their maisonette over into a studio for her, she painted enthusiastically, and when she entered some of her paintings for an exhibition, they were highly praised. As soon as she got the canvases home, she took them up to her studio, turned them to the wall and never looked at them again. She painted furiously, a fresh crop, but dissatisfied, threw them into a skip in the road. She spent less and less time in her studio, went back to drifting aimlessly through the city, beside the river, always looking down into the murky stream rather than up at the skyline. And that was really what she was, a passive creature who watched life pass her by. He loved her, but he saw her for what she was. Lord knows he'd had time enough to reflect. That's why it made him laugh to watch this heroic effort to save her. All these great brains, the greatest in the world ('I include you, Dr Newman, I've read up on you'), coming together to save this one worthless sliver of humanity. This creature who had controlled nothing in her own life but who, since her accident, which had also been beyond her control, had been mysteriously transformed into a goddess, a being with unique and special talents, who was treated reverently by all around her. By all except him, that is, the man who loved her.

A gust of wind stirred the branches of the elm over our heads, and sent a couple of leaves tumbling down. Levy caught one and tore it viciously in two.

'I, for one, refuse to climb into her coffin with her,' he blurted out angrily. Then he turned his head away, so that I couldn't see his face.

We sat in silence for a moment or two. I found that I felt sorry for him. I would have liked to say something, to show him that I understood, but I was afraid that anything I said at that moment would provoke an emotional outburst in him: tears, perhaps, or anger. When he spoke again, however, I saw that he was quite calm. He was a father now, he said, and not a husband. He had grieved for long enough and he considered his marriage to be over and himself a free man. But he was also compassionate. Soon his son would be old enough to accompany him on his travels. He couldn't countenance the idea of abandoning Diane, however little was left of her, so he wanted to set her free too. And on that note, he said, raising his face to mine, he had some good news.

'My petition has gone to the Court of Appeal. My lawyer thinks it has a good chance.'

I felt a little tide of nausea rise in my stomach. 'I wish you would reconsider,' I said quietly. 'I really think there's hope.'

Levy cocked his head and looked at me with such bright, curious eyes that I averted my own. Then he asked me patiently, in the sort of voice he might have reserved for his infant son, if something had happened that he should know about; if there had been a development in the experiment. I shifted in my seat and shook my head. It was simply a feeling I had, an intuition, that his wife was alive and would soon make the fact known to us.

He continued to look at me in that strange, inquisitive way, so that I was caught off guard by his next question.

'Who was it, who died?'

I stiffened. He turned to face me fully, hiking one elbow over the back of the bench. 'An old man who hears voices, a woman who sees ghosts,' he said, his dark eyes blazing, his nose close to mine, 'they have *intuitions*. But you, Sarah, what drives you?'

A long silence stretched between us. Then suddenly I laughed. 'You do!'

He frowned, not understanding.

'Wasn't it you who signed the consent form?' I asked, in mock innocence.

He curled his lip in disgust and turned away. I watched

him closely, I was learning to be wary of him, and sure enough a few minutes later his mood had changed again. Tipping his head back, pouting into the clear, spring air above his head, he pronounced Mezzanotte's name a few times. He sounded out the syllables in a slow, menacing tone, reminding me of a wolf limbering up to howl. His Adam's apple bobbed down behind the yellowish, elastic skin of his throat, then up again, to disappear behind the thick black growth of his beard. Then he brought his head forward abruptly and turned to me.

'Does the name Kalb mean anything to you?' he asked.

'Of course,' I replied, without thinking.

Kalb was the young student from East Germany who received a special dispensation to work in Mezzanotte's lab for a summer, all those years ago, and who helped him conduct that famous series of sleep experiments. What happened to him after that, I couldn't say. Perhaps he went to America. Perhaps he made his name in another field. Levy was watching me intently now, from under level eyebrows, and then he told me that he had done a little homework on 'this character Kalb'.

He had tracked him down to a sordid bedsit in Heidelberg. He was a ruined man who suffered from a whole raft of medical conditions brought on by high blood pressure. A broken creature whom fate had beaten and beaten, until he could not have been brought any lower, but who still dreamed of the revenge he would take on the man who had abandoned him to that fate. Abandoned him, what's more, in the name of science. The man who, when he, Kalb, returned to his home behind the Iron Curtain, lured back there by a death in the family, and had his scribblings confiscated by the Stasi, lifted not a finger to help, but turned his back on him and claimed sole ownership of the precious data they had collected together. Kalb spent time in a prison cell, was set free, and in the years that followed carved out a meagre living for himself as a schoolteacher, returning intermittently to the police cell. When the Wall came down, he went to Heidelberg and found work as a technician at the medical school, hoping to make a fresh start. Very quickly his health started to fail, the years of abuse caught up with him and he wound up in a bedsit, an invalid with nobody to care for him.

I listened to all this in silence. 'None of us knows what really happened,' I murmured, at last. That was true, Levy said, but Kalb had made a few friends during his time at the university, and they remembered that shameful episode. Some of them now held positions of authority in the institution, and they had decided that justice should be done, even if it was too late for Kalb.

I stood up. 'Goodbye, Mr Levy,' I said. He stared at me, and then something in him seemed to snap. His head sank forward, his arms hung limply between his knees. In his crumpled desert fatigues and dusty boots he could have passed for a tramp himself. I turned away and came face to face with the little boy, Conrad. The look in his eye made me start. It was a knowing and very adult look. On his cheek was a dusting of pollen, and in his plump fist he held a posy of snowdrops. I sidestepped him and walked off quickly along the path. When I had gone a little way I stopped to look back. Levy had gathered the child on to his knee and was burying his face in his hair, kissing him all over his face. As the boy squirmed in his lap, the father tossed his head back and I saw that his cheeks were wet with tears. But the boy didn't take his eyes off me, and I felt his solemn stare burning a hole between my shoulder blades as I walked away, and for a long time afterwards.

16

I dreamed lucidly that night, in full colour and, apparently, sound. My dream had a thread, a logic even, though both familiar and unfamiliar elements weaved in and out of it. When I woke in the morning I remembered it in all its awful clarity. I was able to see it for what it was, that is, the reworking by my imagination of the raw material of the past few days, and the overlaying on to that material of the plot of a film I had seen a few weeks earlier, one night after finishing late at the hospital.

The story of the film, and so of the dream, was as follows: a young couple making a long car trip stopped at a petrol station. The man, who showed a striking resemblance to Levy, filled the tank while the woman, who was tall and slim, with cropped dark hair and large brown eyes, went into the shop. After paying he waited for her in the car. When, after some time, she failed to return, he went in to find her. The sales assistant remembered her coming in (she was beautiful), but hadn't noticed her emerge from the lavatories. The young man pushed open the door and called her name. No answer. He quizzed a woman coming out, but she only shrugged her shoulders. He searched the empty stalls himself. With a growing sense of unease he shouted for her in the shop, on the forecourt, in the parking lot behind the building and finally from the grass verge, the din of the traffic drowning out his cries.

After many hours, in shock and sadness, he continued his journey. The police were called but found no clues. His own search continued for weeks, which stretched into months and then years. He simply had to know what happened to her, he couldn't rest until he knew the truth. One day, after several years had passed, he received a letter telling him, 'I know where your girlfriend is. Meet me at [the anonymous correspondent named a café] and you'll find out. Call the police and you'll always live in doubt.'

The young man rushed to the rendezvous, and found himself face to face with a balding, middle-aged man, a timid travelling salesman type who sported thick glasses just like those of Professor Harding. 'Well?' he demanded. 'What have you done with her?'

The salesman smiled diffidently. He had come to offer to take the young man to her. 'Let's go,' said the young man, jumping to his feet. The salesman looked up at him. 'It's not that simple,' he explained, regretfully. 'I can't just take you there. The only way it will happen is if you trust me. You must agree to take a sleeping draught. When you wake up, you will be in the same place as your girlfriend. At long last, you will be reunited with her.'

The young man stared down at him, then impulsively reached out and bunched the man's shirt front in his fist. 'If you hit me,' the salesman explained in the same melancholy tone, 'I'll call the manager. You'll be charged with bodily harm and you'll have thrown away your one chance of peace.' In despair the young man released him, sat down and agreed to take the draught. When he woke some time later, he found himself lying on his back in a small, enclosed space in pitch darkness. A womb-like darkness in which all he could hear was the frenetic beat of his own heart. Flicking a cigarette lighter, he saw that he was in a coffin. All around him was the damp smell of soil.

I woke from this dream around five, in a lather of sweat. My head ached and my throat was parched. 'Flu,' I said to myself, 'Perhaps I won't go in today.' I fell back into a dreamless sleep. When I woke again a few hours later, I had no fever and I decided there was nothing to keep me at home. I set off with a bad taste in my mouth, like a remnant of the dream, and there was an idea I couldn't get out of my head: that only a few weeks earlier, I had been convinced that Diane was bored with the experiment. As if ennui was likely to be the most pressing concern of a living creature incarcerated in a glass coffin. Ashamed at this failure of my imagination, at my inability to see the world through her eyes, I hung my head and dragged my feet. I reached the hospital anyway and took the lift to the fifth floor. At the mouth of the corridor, I hesitated. The rhythmic sound of the machines reached me as usual, but now there seemed to me something reproachful in that sound. An accusation. I walked on, averting my eyes from the open doorways from which emanated the sinister suck and sigh of the ventilators. I didn't look but I muttered to myself, like an amulet, pertinent facts about each patient as I passed his or her cell. 'X, a broken heart, not long to go now . . . Y, very young, an overdose . . .'

At the second turn in the corridor I halted in surprise. A beam slanting down out of the very last room, an intense shaft of light that seemed to me too bright, too golden for daylight, but not artificial either, struck the opposite wall of the corridor near its base. I hurried towards it. As I approached the second to last room the murmur of voices distracted me, and slowing down I glanced in. A doctor and several nurses, all in white, stood huddled round the bed, so that I couldn't see the patient. I caught a glimpse of the doctor bending over him, shaking him, calling out his name urgently. 'Mr Aziz! Mr Aziz!' One of the nurses, a new girl I didn't recognise, saw me and drew the curtain around the bed. I walked on, more slowly now, towards the light which seemed to fade with each step I took. As I turned in at the doorway I was confronted by another strange sight: John Wraith at the far side of the bed, his frame looming large and broad against the window. The watery sunbeam that entered the room illuminated the white hair which fanned out over his shoulders, transforming it into a sort of halo. His blue eyes, blind as they were, seemed to grope their way towards the bed's occupant, and on his lips was a wild, ecstatic smile.

When I asked him what had happened he could only shake his head and press his lips together, as if trying to form a word. I looked at Diane, but there was nothing different about her that I could discern. Her pretty, dark head lay on the pillow, her lazy gaze rolled across the ceiling and her mouth was twisted into its familiar sardonic smile – as if she were sucking on lemons, it occurred to me, out of the blue. Perhaps there was something new about the tilt of her head, the shape of her brow, something attentive, as if she were listening to what was going on in the next room, but I don't think so. I helped the old man to sit down and perched on the bed facing him. His breath came in great shudders, his ribcage heaved. He rambled a bit and I leaned forward to catch his words. I didn't understand what he was trying to tell me and when I said so, he struck his thigh with his fist in frustration.

I spoke soothingly to him until his breathing steadied, then asked him again what had happened in the room. 'Mind your own business,' he muttered. I sat up, startled. Then I told him, sharply, that Levy expected a decision from the Appeal Court any day now, and he was confident it would be in his favour. The old man's eyes darted from side to side like those of a whipped animal, and he found his voice. He had arrived that morning to find a commotion going on in the next room, he said – a medical crisis of some sort. He overheard one of the nurses saying that old Aziz had contracted a virulent infection, and that in his condition it would certainly be terminal. It upset him, partly because deaths were still unusual events on the ward. But far more worrying, in his eyes, was that Aziz's departure would leave a vacancy next to his daughter's room, when by rights the occupant of the first room on the corridor, the one nearest the nurse's station, should vacate first. It didn't seem right to him that the heartbroken widower lingered on, while the relatively robust Aziz had succumbed to an infection and would soon die. He heard them say that antibiotics were useless against it. What was this terrible infection, and where had it come from? The whole thing seemed to signify some upset at the core of the organism; some deep, organic trouble. It was not in the natural order of things, and he didn't like it. He didn't like it at all.

He rushed into Diane's room, thinking she would be upset. He tried to pretend everything was as normal and set to massaging her hands, only to find that there was no stiffness in them at all. To his astonishment, and for the first time since he had started visiting her, they were quite supple. The sun must have been shining into the room. He revelled in his own physical sensations: the warmth of the sun through the shirt on his back, the pleasure of massaging lithe, lissom muscles, the softness of the skin on the backs of her hands. Very soon he had put the shock of Aziz's illness behind him. He concentrated on the steady rhythm of his actions and gradually allowed himself to be lulled into a sort of trance. It was then that she spoke to him. She used the method they had refined between them, that is, she didn't speak with her lips and tongue, though he understood her as clearly as if she had. Her voice rang out like a bell in his head.

First she told him how pleased she was that he had come, which surprised him as he sat with her every morning. Then she started to describe a journey. At first he didn't understand. Whose journey was it? It soon dawned on him that she was describing her own impressions – that she was the traveller – and he grew anxious. Perhaps she was delirious, perhaps she was coming down with the bug? He got up, intending to fetch a nurse, but she asked him to sit down again and reassured him that she was not ill. She continued to describe her journey and he listened, increasingly humble and amazed.

It had started in a gallery in Florence, where his wife had suggested she and Levy spend their honeymoon. Something happened to her while she was in that gallery to make her see the world differently. A sort of revelation, he gathered. After that there were various adventures – the kind of adventures that befall travellers. She had gone away, far away, she had changed as a result of her accumulated experiences and now she had returned, a different person. She wasn't sure how long she had been away – a few months, a year at the most. She was so pleased to find him there to greet her, him of all people, because she knew that he must have been on a similar odyssey of his own. For a time, she imagined, he was torn between two worlds. Then waking one morning to find himself at last, completely blind, he was ushered definitively into the new world. That world was one he felt through other senses. To begin with it seemed a new and different place, it terrified him. Gradually he learned to find his way in it, he ventured further afield, and soon it would become as dear and familiar to him as the old world. Speechless, he nodded to show her he had understood. 'That's just how it was with me,' he said, hoarsely, shaking his head in wonder. According to her, then, they were in the same boat, father and daughter. Both were travellers, both were nearing their final destination, their 'place in the sun'. Once they had reached it, they wouldn't leave it again. They would be at peace.

He stopped talking and closed his eyes. I glanced at Diane. Her head lay on the pillow as before, her expression hadn't changed. I asked him where it was, this warm, sunny spot. The old man's mouth gaped, revealing the yellowish-brown pegs of his lower incisors, and he shut his mouth again. He seemed suddenly overcome with emotion. His eyes grew moist, large tears splashed on to his cheeks and with his great fist he smeared the salty fluid away. He didn't know. Bleary-eyed, the same ecstatic smile playing around his lips, he staggered to his feet and took a deep breath, swelling his ribcage.

With the tears still clinging to his cheeks, he demanded in a passionate roar to see the director of the hospital. His arms flailed about him. He wouldn't be put off. He would tell her what had happened and he would ask her to inform the court, so that Levy's petition could be thrown out and his daughter's future safeguarded. He broke off suddenly, panting. Then under his breath, as if arguing with himself, he mumbled, 'It's under his nose, but the boy doesn't see.' Lifting his great head to the window, he stood there as still as a statue. I caught my breath as a cloud parted from the sun and the milky discs of his irises shone brilliantly. After a moment, he turned his head partly back towards me and his features crumpled into a frown.

'Are you there?'

'Yes,' I assured him, 'I'm still here.'

He asked me for directions to the director's office, and after a moment's confusion I realised that I didn't know where it was myself. I had received letters from that place, memos via the internal mail bearing the director's signature, and I had seen her name, along with all the learned letters after it, printed in block capitals on a board by the front door. I had even seen her quoted in the newspapers, but as far as I knew, I had never laid eyes on her. I had never heard her voice nor penetrated her office, and now that I came to think about it, the latter was not even indicated on the white signpost in the entrance hall.

The old man laughed genially. 'Well, it can't be higher than us now. We're at the top!'

He was right. She wasn't to be found at the top of the north wing, where one might naturally expect her to be, because that space had been thoroughly invaded by the sickest patients. The first few floors were given over to administration, hygiene, catering and consulting rooms, while the basement received no natural light. The third floor was a possibility, especially with all the renovations and upheaval going on there, but still, I had never knowingly seen her there.

I laughed, embarrassed, and the old man, gazing at the floor, smiled in sympathy. I scratched my head. The juvenile and geriatric wings were smaller, the nursing staff of each shared a single common room and they would certainly know if the director toiled in their midst. Only the north wing was sufficiently large that one could assume a person worked there without ever actually seeing her, or being able to point to the physical space she occupied. This is crazy, I said to myself. Where on earth is the director hiding herself, along with all her deputies and secretarial staff?

By now the old man had buttoned himself into his brown mac, pulled up the collar and balanced a black beret on his unruly hair. Grasping his cane in his left hand, he wandered over to the sideboard. The window at his back, he trailed the knuckles of his right hand over the objects that littered it. After a moment I shook my head, admitted defeat and suggested he ask at the nurse's station on his way out. The next time we met, he could tell me what he had found out.

He nodded, amused, and at that moment his fingers came into contact with the bowl of cotton reels. His smile vanished, the muscles of his face grew taut and his mouth hardened into a grim line. Digging his hand in, he removed a reel wound with bright yellow cotton, weighed it in his palm and slipped it into the pocket of his coat. I saw all this dimly, barely grasping what it meant, but the old man seemed not to be aware that he had been observed. Or perhaps he didn't know what he had done. His expression relaxed again and he walked towards the door, turning as he did so to blow a kiss to his daughter. The gesture threw him off his line so that he shouldered the doorpost on his way out, swung round it into the corridor and vanished from sight. At that moment I understood that he was the thief; that he really existed and his wife hadn't imagined it. I felt a kind of chill grip me and I sat quite still on the bed, listening to the tap-tap of his cane as it receded down the corridor.

17

The door swung back to reveal a large, sunlit room into which the noise of the outside world did not penetrate. It was a brilliant but cold day in early April. Dust motes floated tranquilly in the rays that slanted down from three sash windows, windows I had once gazed up at from outside, from a courtyard encircled by marble columns. Back then I had half expected to find those rays slanting on to the broad shoulders of Mezzanotte, as he looked up from his magnificent, gold-inlaid desk. Now I hovered uncertainly in the doorway, surveying a very different scene.

In front of me, stretching lengthwise from left to right, was a long rectangular table with a highly polished surface. On the far side, facing me, sat two men and a woman. Mezzanotte sat opposite them, presenting his back to me. All wore black, but the woman's shiny brown hair was pulled back from her forehead and temples into a tight chignon. She alone looked up and smiled as I entered. She must have been about my age. The secretary who had opened the door to me announced me, and indicated the empty chair at one end of the table.

I sat down and tried to catch Mezzanotte's eye. He continued to stare ahead of him, his hands clasped in his lap, sitting languidly across his chair. His posture expressed a profound boredom, and I looked at him with a mixture of fear and admiration. The lines that ran down from the corners of his eyes, the guy ropes as I thought of them, seemed to accentuate the ageing flesh. In the mirror-like surface of the table swam a foreshortened, inverted image of his long face, his noble brow and wistful brown eyes, which gazed far off into the distance. The reflected faces of the panel members, in contrast, were obscured by piles of papers, in the margins of which they now scribbled.

In the silence, broken only by the scrawl of pencil on paper, I waited to find out why I had been summoned. At last the man nearest me looked up, the chairman perhaps. A white-haired, distinguished-looking gentleman with coal-black eyebrows and a black moustache, he told me that I was merely required to explain or corroborate any scientific statements the professor might make, and to provide extra details where necessary. I glanced at the professor out of the corner of my eye, saw him raise his chin by the tiniest fraction. The chairman then spoke to him with the utmost charm and courtesy.

'Thank you, Professor, for explaining so clearly the theory behind your clever device. Please be kind enough to tell to us, now, what went wrong in the cases of Patients AC and BK.'

The professor gazed at the chairman with the weary, almost affectionate look of a warrior confronting an ancient foe. I raised a finger, intending to protest that I knew nothing about those particular patients and so couldn't advise the panel. The chairman smiled obliquely at me and bade me let the professor speak. And speak he did, with perfect poise and self-assurance, as if addressing a ceremony at which he were about to be rewarded for his life's work.

He began with the story of Patient BK. This, it seems, was a man in his early fifties who, following a brain haemorrhage, was diagnosed as suffering from locked-in syndrome. A car park attendant, BK had always boasted of having an unusually high IQ. His family, desperate to help him, had clung to this claim and offered it up as evidence that BK would make an ideal subject for the professor. The professor, being short of willing subjects, was inclined to give him the benefit of the doubt. BK was trained to use the Mind-Reading Device, to modulate his slow cortical potentials, and it turned out that he had not exaggerated. He learned so quickly that the psychologist working with him was able to move him on to the alphabet after only a month. At that point, however, his progress slowed to a snail's pace. Worried, the psychologist reported the development to Mezzanotte, who paid the patient a visit during one of his training sessions. By asking questions to which the patient was able to reply with one blip of the cursor for yes, two for no, the psychologist got to the bottom of the mystery. BK was illiterate. A truant throughout his school years, he had never learned to read or write. The professor was furious, nowhere was this mentioned in his records. But that, BK managed to explain, was because he had lied about it all his life.

The professor fell silent, but did not take his eyes off the chairman. The woman, who had nodded encouragingly at me when she had seen me raise my finger, and had seemed to listen sympathetically to the professor's tale, now leaned forward and pointed the tip of her pencil at him.

'So the experiment was, in fact, a spectacular failure?' she said, fixing him with her shrewd, hazel eyes.

The professor threw her a disdainful glance. 'On the contrary, madam . . .'

She corrected him: 'Doctor.' Dipping his head slightly to acknowledge his error, he continued to address her coldly.

'On the contrary, Doctor, I consider it a resounding success.' With that he turned back to the chairman. 'It naturally annoyed me that BK would never learn to operate the machine in the way I had intended, and that he had kept his illiteracy a secret, so I informed him there and then that I was dropping him from the programme . . .'

The woman and the second man exchanged glances. I saw it and held my breath. Mezzanotte, oblivious to all of us except the chairman, continued with his story:

He had got up to leave, but by means of some frantic signalling, BK managed to attract his attention and to persuade him to stay a few minutes longer. More laborious questioning followed, from which it transpired that he had his own ideas about how the machine could help him. Mezzanotte listened, reluctantly at first, then with growing interest. He went away and adapted the technology according to BK's wishes. The patient was now happy; a self-confessed 'liberated man'. He regarded himself as a connoisseur of the female form, and he now spent his days browsing the vast electronic library that existed on the subject, and that his newly acquired skills had at last put at his disposal.

'Porn?' the brown-haired woman asked, in a strident voice.

'Exactly that, madam,' the professor replied, and gave her a watery smile. She looked him up and down, tapped her pencil once sharply on her notepad and sat back. The chairman took up the questioning.

'Patient AC was a woman, I believe?'

Yes, the professor confirmed, AC was a housewife and an altogether more unfortunate case. Within a year of being diagnosed with motor neurone disease she was breathing with the aid of a ventilator. It was the nature of that particular disease that while the muscles wasted, the mind continued to function normally. The ocular muscles were the last to go, so for a long time AC was able to signal what she wanted by blinking with her left eyelid. She was a garrulous woman by nature, and to begin with her friends flocked to see her at the hospital. She communicated with them by winking furiously, she even made them laugh with her black humour. Then the last vestige of muscular control slipped away from her, and from one moment to the next she was silenced. Her friends continued to visit her, but gradually their visits became shorter, then fewer, until finally they stayed away altogether. Even her husband stopped coming. He found it hard to believe she was still 'in there', or perhaps he couldn't bring himself to face the fact that she was, and as talkative and fond of company as ever. That prospect was too horrible for him to contemplate. It was nevertheless true, and this was the predicament AC found herself in when the professor turned up to meet her doctors and to assess her for inclusion in the experimental programme.

'I imagine you found her an enthusiastic student,' said the second man, drily.

Mezzanotte seemed not to notice his questioner's tone. Yes, he concurred, she had also learned quickly. Because, unlike BK, she had been conscientious at school and had a good command of the alphabet, she was churning out words within a matter of weeks. Then short sentences. The trouble was . . . and here he threw me a sidelong glance which made my blood run cold. I felt as if I were sitting in the stalls of a packed theatre, looking up at the stage, watching someone close to me falter and forget his lines.

'Nobody could have foreseen . . .' he said, waving his hand in a gesture of helplessness. 'It was beyond my control . . .'

All three members of the committee leaned forward in their seats. The professor paused, flexed his fingers and re-clasped them on his knee. He took a deep breath and cleared his throat. I bit my lip, I willed him on. The trouble was, he continued, that by now it was already March. AC hadn't had a visitor all winter. Her husband had gone to Spain. The staff did what they could, they tried to persuade her old friends to visit, but no-one was interested. They had nothing to say to her after so long. So she lay in her room, wired up to the apparatus, staring at the ceiling and waiting for the knock that meant company. It never came. In the end, with the help of the machine, she wrote a short note to the professor. She thanked him for his efforts and asked that he switch it off. Then she turned her face to the wall, and a week later she was dead.

As the three members of the panel set to scribbling again, and the silence in the room lengthened, I fell back in my chair, limp, aghast at the thought of Patient AC, who had become cut off from the world even while she was still in it. It reminded me of another story I had heard a few weeks earlier, from an elderly patient who had come to my attention because he suffered from an unusual, creeping form of amnesia. A war veteran, he reminisced throughout my interview with him, frantically, as if he had to rehearse the few memories that were left to him to keep them alive; as if, without them, he would be lost.

Just before he left the old man told me one last tale. During the war with Japan, he had commanded a platoon that was taken prisoner and put to work in the mines under Nagasaki Bay. One day, the mine they were in started to flood. Rats appeared from nowhere and debris poured down the shaft. He realised the shaft must be cleared, and quickly, or they would all be buried alive. He gave orders and his men went to work, standing on each other's shoulders, digging and scraping their way out. They reached the surface at first light on an August morning and looked around them. Nagasaki had vanished. A tidal wave had been through, and a typhoon. Their former prison camp had been flattened; the ground on which it had stood was littered with corpses. No human being had survived the cataclysm that had taken place while they were trapped underground, and whose origin was a mystery to them. The landscape was dripping and covered with mud. The world had changed beyond all recognition.

I raised my head and met the enquiring gaze of the woman.

'In your professional opinion,' she asked me, 'could AC's death have been avoided?'

I pulled myself up in my chair. 'Oh no, I don't think so . . . I mean, I can't comment, never having met . . .' I stammered on, the blood rising to my cheeks, aware that the two men on the panel were whispering behind their hands while Mezzanotte continued to stare ahead of him. I paused, took a deep breath, collected my thoughts and began again. 'That is, it's true that such a patient might be psychologically rather, er . . . fragile and ah . . . might need help adjusting to her new circumstances. But her death avoided? No, I wouldn't say so.'

'Thank you,' said the woman. The second man then broke off his whispering and addressed me. 'That's very interesting, what you just said. Of course it's plain common sense. Even very able people need help adjusting to new and frightening situations. Tell me, Dr Newman, did you know a young man named Franz Kalb?'

A chill ran down my spine. 'Franz Kalb went home of his own accord,' I murmured, but the man asked me to speak up. He couldn't hear. So I raised my voice, and this time I was unable to keep the anger out of it. 'Franz Kalb went home of his own accord. Professor Mezzanotte made every effort to persuade him to stay, but his mind was made up. There was nothing more the professor could have done . . .'

My voice trailed off as Mezzanotte turned his dull gaze on me. I didn't have time to worry about him, though, because now I was the centre of attention and the questions were coming at me thick and fast.

18

I hadn't wanted to leave Mezzanotte alone in the room, but I had no choice. After the panel had concluded its inquisition the chairman dismissed me, so I sat down to wait for him on a bench at the bottom of the wide sweep of stairs. A clock ticked in the hall, minutes passed but still there was no footstep above me. For the first time I really felt afraid for the professor. I ran over the answers I had given in my head, but as far as I could see the questions referred to matters over which he had no control, or incidents for which he could in no way be held responsible. For instance, at one point they asked me to describe a day in the life of Patient DL. I did so, but what possible bearing could that have on his case?

At around seven thirty, I began, a nurse enters and draws the curtains. She washes the patient with a flannel and warm water, eases the pressure points to prevent bedsores and generally takes care of basic hygiene. She also turns on the television, which remains on until lights out in the evening – though the patient's father turns the volume right down while he is visiting, the better to hear himself think.

He is the first visitor of the day. He arrives at nine and massages her hands which tend to be in spasm. As soon as he's gone I come in to set up my equipment. I give the patient her lesson, following the same procedure each day. As I'm packing up, sometimes before I've quite finished, Mrs Wraith arrives. That's the patient's mother. She usually brings something new for DL to wear, or an ornament to brighten up the room, and she talks without drawing breath. She thinks that the sound of her voice is stimulating for her daughter, and there are grounds for believing she's right.

The patient's mother may stay for anything from half an hour to three hours. After she's gone a junior doctor drops by, Dr Bartholomew calls in every few days and of course the nurses check on her regularly. There is the occasional visit from the physiotherapist, the hairdresser and the dental hygienist. Other than that the patient is left to herself. The only uncertainty in her life is the irregular visits of her husband. Once a week, sometimes once a month, he comes by. He doesn't stay long, a quarter of an hour perhaps. Then a nurse looks in again, gives her the second of her two daily doses of insulin, checks everything is in order and turns out the lights. That, presumably, is when she sleeps.

So far so good. But at that point the woman piped up and asked me if I could be sure that the patient slept. 'Yes,' I replied, 'even if it's not obvious from looking at her. Whether she dreams is another matter.'

I don't know why I added that last part, perhaps because I had wondered it so often myself. Anyhow, as I said it the second man on the panel raised his head and looked at me with interest. I felt nervous at the prospect of answering another question from him and it may have showed, because he spoke to me gently. He was full of admiration for the members of my profession, he said, who worked tirelessly to improve the lives of those less fortunate than themselves, et cetera, et cetera . . . but as a layman he was also acutely aware that in the blink of an eye – if I would pardon the expression – he could find himself in the same predicament as DL: trapped in a glass coffin, as a previous witness had so vividly and terrifyingly put it to the tribunal. What he wanted to know was, didn't I consider such an existence rather monotonous? Or, if he could put the question another way, surely what made life worth living was its very variety, its unpredictability. He would be grateful if I would spell it out for him: what distinguished one day from the next, in the extraordinary life of Patient DL?

I thought about it and then answered very carefully, with the caveat that it was naturally impossible to gauge a mute patient's view of her own life. 'Yes, yes,' he interjected, with a hint of impatience, 'that goes without saying.'

'Well,' I continued, 'if you ask me what distinguishes one day from the next for Patient DL, I would have to say honestly that it is nothing more than the colour of her nail varnish, or the fact that she is wearing a new blouse.'

My questioner nodded, and the corner of his mouth twitched. Then the chairman asked me, 'Does she know what season it is?'

That one I found easier to answer. 'Not unless one of her visitors happens to mention it. You see, the light level is carefully controlled in the hospital. The windows are never opened on the wards and the temperature fluctuates only by fractions of a degree.' I was about to add that seasons were a dim memory for DL, if she was able to remember at all, but I bit my tongue. Instead I said, 'Of course, once she has learned to use the professor's machine she will be able to ask what month it is, and receive an answer.'

Once again they all set to scribbling and soon after that I was dismissed. Sitting in the empty hall, I congratulated myself on that last flash of inspiration. In hindsight it was the obvious thing to say. Still, the more I went over what had passed between me and the panel, the more I felt a sort of growing resentment. I got to my feet once, intending to march back into the room and set the record straight, but I sat down again, not knowing exactly what I would say. The clock ticked on. I had waited an hour already and another half-hour passed before I heard a step above me. I raised my eyes to the figure standing in front of me and blurted out angrily, 'What do they want from you?' Mezzanotte looked down at me with a peculiarly fine and painful smile. Under the high ceiling, beside the grand, sweeping staircase, he suddenly appeared shrunken, an old man weighed down by the world. 'I'd like to see Patient DL,' he said. 'Perhaps there is something I can do for her.'

We walked back to the hospital. He didn't refer to what had happened in the room after I left it and I didn't ask. But I noticed, with a contraction of my heart, that he wasn't in a hurry. Ever since I had known him, Mezzanotte had been impatient to get back to some experiment or other. Now he strolled at a leisurely pace, his hands in his pockets, like a man who has just been fired and, still in a state of shock, is revelling in the pleasure of not being expected anywhere. He even whistled a snatch of something, *The Queen of the Night*'s aria, I think it was.

I racked my brains for something to say to distract him from his thoughts. Then it occurred to me, the piece of news that would cheer him up. Except that it wasn't exactly news, and in the light of what had happened I was ashamed I had kept it from him for so long. So anyhow, I broke the news to Mezzanotte that there was at least a glimmer of hope in the case of Patient DL. She, like his other two students, had managed to harness her slow cortical potentials to the extent of moving the cursor in the desired direction, and of sending the Pac-Man flying towards its alimentary target. Mezzanotte stopped and turned towards me, frowning.

'It worked, you say?'

Yes, I confirmed, laughing, as excited as if I had just made the discovery myself: Patient DL had made the machine work! But, and here I stopped smiling, and spoke almost sternly to him, she had only made it work once – or rather, three times in the same day, and then not again. I had kept the development to myself, I explained, because I considered it parsimoniously as a single result, and one that had not been repeated. Although I personally did not believe it to be an artefact, without replication on another day I could not really prove that it wasn't. Even if it was real, our patient seemed at least superficially to have lost the will to carry on. She had gone quiet, and for that there were various possible explanations. There may be side effects we didn't know about, headaches or nausea, or perhaps the effort required of her was simply too great.

Mezzanotte listened to all this in silence. He stroked his chin. He took a few rapid steps along the pavement and returned. 'I'll look into it!' he said, and pointed a forefinger at the sky. We moved off again, the professor taking longer, more purposeful strides now. As we emerged from the cobbled tunnel that connected the outside world to the square, the front steps of the hospital came into view with Nestor at the top of them, leaning back against the red brick, smoking a cigarette and watching through narrowed eyes the human traffic that entered and left through the great portal.

The professor strode up the steps, taking them two at a time. 'To work, man!' he cried, pointing with his whole arm into the hospital's gaping, black mouth. Nestor, removing the stub of his cigarette from where it was glued to his lip, eyed him mutinously. The professor passed into the entrance hall, but I paused long enough to challenge Nestor with a look of my own. He threw his stub on to the pavement, saluted me and, with a click of his heels, said in a whining voice, 'Nothing to report, ma'am.'

I caught up with Mezzanotte at the lift. He was, by now, thoroughly agitated. He had been wrong to neglect DL, he said, not to keep a close eye on proceedings so that at the slightest step forward, or back, he could make adjustments to the device and in that way, so to speak, smooth her path back to life. He was to blame, he had spread himself too thin. He wouldn't make the same mistake again. He would watch this one like a hawk, he would not leave her side (metaphorically speaking), he would bring her slowly but surely, by the use of stick and carrot, to the threshold of speech and on into a happy and productive future. He would prove his device, come what may.

We entered the long corridor on the fifth floor almost at a run. As we reached the second turn we heard angry voices and slowed our step. The voices grew louder as we approached Diane's room, the professor and I glanced at each other, and we turned into the last room on the corridor to find it crowded with people.

The patient lay in her bed, docile, her sleepy gaze sliding past her visitors as if they were figures in a dream. A few paces beyond the end of the bed, Denise Wraith and Levy stood, nose to nose, fists clenched, red-faced. In the corner by the window, John Wraith stood with his arms folded over his chest, his head bowed like a penitent.

The professor happened to enter first and demanded to know what was going on. Levy, who had his back to us, turned on him furiously. 'Keep out of it,' he growled. 'I know all about you, so you'd better watch out.'

Having rendered the professor momentarily speechless, he turned back to his adversary, who was regarding him with a triumphant sneer.

'Threats now, is it?' she snorted.

John Wraith raised his head at the sound of the new element in the room and I saw that his face was mottled and shiny with perspiration. Trailing his knuckles along the edge of the cluttered sideboard, he moved nimbly across the room towards the fighting pair. When he was parallel with the foot of the bed, he turned in towards them and reached out to grip their upper arms. In surprise and irritation, they turned towards him. He was breathing hard. He looked towards the door and asked if I was there. I told him I was. Satisfied, he turned back to Levy and his wife. 'Diane speaks to me,' he said. 'Only to me. It's a sort of . . . telepathy we use, as Dr Newman is my witness. And . . . ah, wait, she's talking to me right now. Shhh, yes! She wishes you wouldn't fight. She's happy, she says, she has found her place in the sun!'

With his head tipped back, his lips slightly parted and his eyes sliding from side to side, as if he really were extracting something from the ether, he stood there, anchored by their two upper arms. There was a stunned silence in the room, which seemed to last for a long time before Denise turned to me with a puzzled frown. 'Is it true?' she asked.

The old man continued to clutch his wife's arm, but now he released Levy's and raised a shaking forefinger to his nose, as if requesting silence. Whether it was so that he could hear what Diane was saying to him, or my reply to his wife's question, I'll never know. The silence stretched on, I didn't know what to say. The old man's shoulders became more rounded, he grimaced, he seemed to shrink and cower in front of them, to drag his wife down by the hold he had on her, until his hand slipped off her elbow and fell heavily to his side. She continued to gaze at him with the same puzzled expression. The professor and I looked on, neither of us dared move, until, his face buried in his beard, Levy snickered.

I held my breath. He laughed again, louder this time, and Denise's mouth twitched at the corners. Then she was laughing too, loud gales of mirth directed into her husband's face, so that he twisted this way and that, raised his hands in front of his face and stumbled back into his corner.

I don't recall everything that followed. I watched it all helplessly from the doorway. I remember the professor attempting to intervene and receiving an uppercut to the chin from Levy, who appeared like a small, sinewy imp in the company of those three giants, and who jumped up and down with rage and hatred. I remember John Wraith making tearful, supplicating gestures to the two adversaries, prancing around the patient's bed in an absurd attempt to shield her, and later, on his knees, pawing at his wife's skirt. I remember the disgusted glance she gave him, and her words: 'You don't look well, John. Go and lie down.' It was the only time she took her eyes from her son-in-law's face. I remember the venom that ebbed and flowed between those two. The strange calm with which they received each accusation and batted it back. Levy borrowed his wife's sardonic smile as Denise spat insults at him for the callous ease with which he had selected another woman, another uterus, to harbour his child, before dismissing her, too, as he had 'all the others'. She added, viciously, that the boy's life might also be in danger if he didn't quickly prove useful to his father. I remember how very strange it was to see her smiling when he said, 'You drove her to it. I see it now. You sent us to Florence. She could never have been happy with me, a mere mortal.' She even nodded as if the thought pleased her, and added that her daughter had never been satisfied in her marriage; that she had realised too late that her husband was a mediocre specimen, and that it wouldn't have surprised her if Diane had fallen into the arms of another man, 'a beautiful creature like her'. I remember grasping the fact that Levy's petition had succeeded and that Diane had four weeks to live; I remember the word 'evil', but not who uttered it, and I remember the chilling look in Denise's eye when she turned to me and said, 'This man is a murderer. Get him out.'

Finally, I remember the sob that escaped Levy as he turned and reeled out of the room, pursued by Mezzanotte. I remember the way that Denise resumed her seat by the bed and calmly straightened the sheet covering her daughter, which had somehow become rumpled. And I remember how she kept her head turned away from us, her eyes fixed on her daughter's slack, expressionless face, as I led a gasping, stumbling John Wraith out of the room.

19

A blip. A lunge of the cursor-Pac-Man towards the cartoon apple and then nothing again. If I counted that long-ago trio of responses as a single, so to speak, movement of her spirit, then this was only the second time I had known her stir in the time the experiment had been running, which was close to three months.

At five to the hour, Denise bustled in as usual. The basket she carried was now so full that she was obliged to use both hands to carry it, and still it swung heavily against her shins. Depositing it with a grunt on to the floor near the rocking chair, she raised both hands to touch her hair and began her daily inspection. Her eagle eye scanned the wall that was festooned with curling photos, yellowing letters and childish drawings. Apparently satisfied that everything was in its place there, she shifted her attention to the sideboard, which now groaned under the weight of its burden. Not an inch of the surface was visible, and her gaze roved backwards and forwards over the bowls of wrapped toffee mints, coloured pens and other baubles in no very systematic way. I watched her as I loosened the vice on the vertical support that held Diane's head in place. She ignored me, of course. But I saw the panic grow in her eyes as she counted the drawing implements, lost track and started again.

'Perhaps if I counted for you?' I asked her, after watching her third attempt fail.

She looked at me gratefully and nodded. My hands clasped behind my back, I stalked the length of the sideboard, not daring to lift my eyes from the jumble of paraphernalia which must surely soon become an obstacle to the medical staff. When I reached the window I turned and stalked back in the opposite direction. In fact, I was playing for time, wondering whether it would be better to tell her that something was missing, or nothing was missing. Out of the corner of my eye I saw her, sitting stiffly in the rocking chair, her hands folded in her lap, staring into the space in front of her.

'I believe a pencil has gone,' I announced after a respectable interval. 'A blue crayon, to be precise.' She didn't move, but her lips worked silently as if she were still counting. Looking round, she thanked me demurely and bent over her bulging basket. After a long time she produced a blue crayon of the same make as the others in the bowl, and crossed to the sideboard to put it in its rightful place. Back in her chair, she now pulled out from the depths of the basket the pot of butter-coloured cream and set to working it into her daughter's hands and arms, talking to her all the while.

I strolled back to the window and, leaning sideways on to the frame, gazed down into the garden, where the cherry trees were now coming into blossom. When she paused to draw breath I took the opportunity to ask after her husband. I hadn't seen him for a week or more, since that terrible scene with Levy. He was 'under the weather', she said in a rather pinched voice, without turning round, and 'not fit to come out'. She started muttering again. Something about name tapes. She wanted to sew name tapes into Diane's clothes, the few good things she had, because one or two garments had gone to the hospital laundry and not returned. Most of the patients on this ward rarely had any visitors, and as a result they were dressed in 'rags'. So she wasn't surprised that good things went astray. I listened for a little while longer, then slipped unnoticed from the room, passing the closed door of the neighbouring one, the last resting place but one of Mr Aziz. This door was now plastered with a large yellow sign bearing, in forbidding black capitals, the word 'Quarantine'.

In my office I picked up the telephone and reported Diane's latest response to Mezzanotte. I reminded him that we only had fourteen days left, that the court had demanded a word from the patient as proof that she was conscious (it wouldn't be satisfied with what it considered 'meaningless' lines on a screen) and I also told him my concerns about Denise. She was overwrought, and this was bringing certain compulsive elements of her personality to light. She had a right to know that her daughter had shown signs of life. On the other hand, I couldn't be sure that in her fragile mental state – and with the court deadline looming – she could support the weight of such knowledge. As I might have expected, the professor didn't see what any of this had to do with his experiment. I pointed out that it was, after all, Denise who had brought the patient to his attention, against the wishes of Adrian Levy. There was silence on the line. Then he suggested we double up the training sessions – one in the morning and one in the evening – and keep all future developments to ourselves. I agreed and rang off.

We launched the new schedule. The risk we took was that of tiring our patient, but to our delight she became more rather than less responsive. To begin with I might see a signal from her in one in every three sessions, then one in every two – that is, once a day under the new regime. There was no doubt now that they were genuine. They came more frequently and closer together, but with the same deadly accuracy she had shown the first time, so that I concluded she was at last gaining some kind of subtle control over her brainwaves, and producing sustained signals that she could manipulate easily. I even thought I perceived certain aspects of her personality showing through – here, after all, was a person who refused to respond until she could respond with a bullseye, who in a different life had been so moved by the sight of David: a perfectionist. Though of course that too could have been a phantom thrown up by the technology, which was new to us all.

The time came when not to see a signal was the exception rather than the rule. Days passed in a patchwork of highs and lows: highs whenever her mental efforts displaced the line, lows when there was nothing to see. I was short of sleep, running on adrenalin, leaving too much of my other work to my long-suffering assistants. A week remained until the court had decreed that Diane's feeding tube should be removed, her insulin withdrawn, and our last remaining subject allowed to die. None of us mentioned it. It was naturally a taboo subject in the hearing of the patient herself. We were acutely aware that the signals of which we had seen so many would still not be sufficient to convince a court: we needed a word from the patient herself, uttered or rather written in English. Of secondary importance but nonetheless weighing heavily between us was the fact that Mezzanotte's own salvation depended on the outcome of this experiment. The truth, as I discovered it from him one night, almost by accident, was that he had been granted a period of grace that came to an end on the day Diane had her lifeline removed. After that his contract would be terminated and he would be asked to leave the university. That, to the committee, seemed a fitting punishment for his accumulated, and to my mind imaginary, crimes.

As far as Diane was concerned, I kept Fleur in the picture. I wanted her to be on the alert to call off the execution, as I had come to think of it, and at the eleventh hour if necessary. She made no comment, merely told me to 'beware clouds' and kept an eye on her charge from a distance. Some of the nurses became rather tearful as the deadline approached. Levy had once again vanished, though where to, nobody knew. More than likely, he couldn't bear to look at his wife whom he had condemned to death. Nestor, having had the situation explained to him, became subdued and industrious. He barely left his station, but kept his gaze glued to the screen and the undulating trace. The first time he saw the line digress from its usual path, leap into the upper half of the screen or dive, he raced up to the fifth floor and appeared in the doorway, breathless, staring at the patient with goggle eyes. After that he couldn't have been more co-operative. Whenever the professor came to check up on the patient, he trailed him up through the hospital like a puppy. He talked with relish of putting the lawyers in their place, of 'wiping the smile off Levy's face', and pestered us like a child about when we could move her on to the next stage: the alphabet.

The professor and I discussed the issue at length and, occasionally, into the small hours of the morning. It was towards the end of one of these sessions that, seated comfortably in one of the armchairs in my office, nursing a tumbler of whisky, he let slip what the committee had decided would be his fate. We passed over it in silence and returned to the more pressing issue of how best to manage Patient DL. But if I needed any evidence that his own future worried him, I found it in our heated debates on that subject. We often traded positions where she was concerned, so that sometimes I would find myself defending the impersonal, scientific argument, while he would stand up for our duty of care and the need to remove the subtler, psychological impediments to the patient's progress. There were good reasons why he had set the threshold at the level he had, he insisted; reasons I would surely appreciate. If the patient was not competent to pick the letters she required to make herself understood, if she found herself generating nonsense, she could easily lose heart. The enormity of the task could overwhelm her and she could slip back inside herself. I was surprised by this very human insight on the part of the professor, and I don't think it was inspired purely by his desire to see the experiment succeed. He had changed since his experience in front of the tribunal. These days he was quieter, more thoughtful. I acknowledged that such a setback was a genuine danger but pointed out that time was short. In the end we reached a compromise: he agreed to slightly lower his threshold.

At last the morning arrived when I was to present Diane with the screen showing two banks of thirteen letters – something I had at times doubted I would ever do. I don't mind saying, my heart was in my mouth. To my horror and dismay, when I entered the last room on the corridor of the fifth floor of the hospital, I found Denise already there – an hour before she was due. There were purple shadows under her eyes, she appeared dazed and, if I was not very much mistaken, she wore the same navy blue dress she had worn the day before.

She was leaning over the bed, struggling to drape Diane's naked torso in what looked like a child's blouse. The pattern in the material was of red ladybirds against a white background. First she shoved one sticklike arm into a sleeve, followed by the other, and then she fastened the pink, plastic buttons up over the wasted frame, the prominent ribs and breastbone and small, surprisingly shrivelled breasts, to the petal-shaped collar. 'A child's blouse over an old woman's body,' I thought to myself, and shivered. The cuffs fell short of Diane's bony wrists, but otherwise it fitted well enough. When Denise had completed this operation, she removed the muslin that was draped over her shoulder and wiped the saliva from her daughter's chin. All of this with her mouth fixed in a grim line.

When at last she stepped back to admire her handiwork, I saw the rocking chair behind her, with the pink mohair blanket rumpled and bunched over one arm.

'Did you sleep here last night, Denise?'

She nodded.

'To catch the thief?'

The same childlike nod.

'And did you?'

She didn't answer. Pressing the tip of her forefinger to her lips, she turned to gaze at the sideboard. Hesitantly, almost coquettishly, she pointed at it, seeming to pick out certain objects from the legions that littered it. After a moment, with a puzzled look, she turned back to me.

'You took a blue crayon, I think?'

'Not exactly,' I said, smiling, and explained how she had got things mixed up.

'Not exactly,' she mumbled, several times over, wringing the muslin between her long fingers, looking vaguely into the space beyond my shoulder. 'What does it mean, not exactly? Does it mean yes, or does it mean no?'

Perhaps my own brain was working slowly due to lack of sleep, but I admit it was only then that I began to feel uneasy. Yet, without fully grasping what was happening, a part of me knew that the seeds of it had been sown much earlier, and that I was really only watching the unfolding of an inevitable conclusion.

I tried to hurry her over the subject: 'It's getting late, Denise, it's time for my lesson.'

She looked at me from under heavy lids and said that she

didn't think there was going to be a lesson today. 'I forbid you to come near my daughter again.'

I argued with her as gently as I could. I broke my own rule and reminded her that there was only a week to go, taking care not to mention in the patient's hearing, at least, what would happen at the end of that week. I asked her if she really wished to take such a drastic step, to throw away her last chance, et cetera, et cetera . . . She covered her face with her hands and a strangled sound came from her throat. I held my breath, afraid I had gone too far. After a minute she took her hands away and my blood froze. On her lips was a malevolent smile.

'Mezzanotte will take over from you,' she announced.

Yes, she continued, nodding, she had decided: the professor would teach her daughter how to use the machine. I explained that the professor was a busy man, that anyway he wasn't trained to work with patients. Her idea could never work . . . I regretted it. In a single articulated gesture, like some magnificent predator, she unravelled her spine and flicked up her head. Fixing me with her raptor-like glare, she twisted her mouth into a snarl and hissed, 'And all your clever training, where has it got us?'

I defended myself. I pointed out that it was a highly experimental technology we were dealing with, there were no guarantees . . . I gabbled on and on. She interrupted me to say that the professor had built the machine, and he knew how to get the most out of it. I stammered, 'But, but . . .' But what could I say? In the end I told myself that it would be wise to let the matter drop. It was not the worst possible outcome, but if I pushed her worse might come. So I agreed to put her proposal to the professor.

The snarl vanished and by some trick of the light she melted back into a soft, feminine form, grieving and dignified. Removing a handkerchief from her pocket she dabbed delicately at her eyes. She was sorry, she said, from behind the crumpled ball of cotton, and she'd soon be all right. Then she met my gaze with a bashful smile. 'I only want my daughter to speak to me,' she said. 'Is that too much for a mother to ask?'

Seating herself by the bed, she pulled out the jar of butter-coloured cream, the one with the sickly sweet smell, and went to work. I glanced at Diane, and back at her. Then I left the room, bitter disappointment welling up inside me.

20

There was a hospital, a sprawling, indestructible edifice that was built according to the principles of Victorian psychiatry, and where the line between life and death was sometimes blurred (and which, for that reason, had variously been compared to a plant, a beehive, a dying old woman). At the heart of the hospital was a garden, a clearing in the secret depths of the organism which nevertheless received sunlight, rain and frost, and where the seasons changed in a predictable way.

I had often looked down on this oasis, this lost echo of the world, but had entered it only once, many years earlier. Now, as we embarked on the final week of our experiment, I found myself drawn there. Every evening, at the time when I knew the professor would be giving his second lesson of the day, I borrowed the key from the head porter and let myself into it. I found it soothing to pass the time beneath the window of the room in which our patient lay, especially now that time itself seemed to have slowed to an excruciating pace.

On the fourth night, that is, with two days to go before

Diane's feeding tube was to be removed, I was sitting in my usual place, on a bench at the end furthest from the door. From there I commanded a view of the whole garden. It was the last day of April, the cherries were in blossom and pink petals scattered the grass that formed triangles between the criss-crossing paths. The white flowers of a magnolia tree stood out like new moons in the gathering dusk, and narcissi, lilac and honeysuckle gave out their delicate night scents, which rose up and dissipated in the city vapours. If I tipped my head back I looked past serried ranks of hospital windows, yellow sodium-lit squares, to the purplish, rectangular stain of sky. I gazed up into that darkening space and thought of the sun inching its way away from us, round to the far side of the planet.

I had been sitting there for perhaps a quarter of an hour when I heard the creak of the door at the other end of the garden as it opened and closed. At first, no one emerged from the shadows cast by the building. Then a soft-footed silhouette detached itself from the gloom and padded towards me, veering from right to left, pausing every now and then under a tree, or by a flower bed, and becoming there strangely stooped. The light from the windows illuminated the garden at its edges but not in the centre. When it was still a little distance from me the figure strayed close enough to the wall that I could see its face. Clutching a few straggly flowers, Levy sat down on the bench to my left. The hand holding the stems relaxed its grip, so that they spilled out on to his lap and one rolled to his feet. He made no attempt to pick it up.

We sat like that for a long time. Neither of us moved or

spoke. When the strains of a guitar drifted down to us from above, the amateurish efforts of a visitor to entertain a patient, Levy stirred and snivelled. We both looked up to the lighted windows above us, but the echo created by the arrangement of walls around that open space confused us, or we were reluctant to look one another in the eye. Either way, I instinctively looked to the right, to the still lighted windows of the operating theatres, while he looked to the left, to where, two floors up, the professor must be bringing to a close his nightly effort to manipulate the machine, to conjure like a magician a string of words from his patient.

The musician hit a false note, stumbled over a phrase, fell silent. Another minute passed but he seemed to have lost heart. He didn't play again. I tried to think of the appropriate words to say to Levy. Before I could do so, he gathered up his meagre bouquet, freshly plucked from the hospital soil, already drooping, and got to his feet. I wanted to go with him. Just then I was afraid of being left alone in the garden. I put out a hand but he was already beyond my reach, so I called to him and the anguished echo of my voice ran wildly round that cloistered space.

He returned quickly and perched himself on the edge of the bench. 'You asked me once who had died,' I said. 'It was my sister. She came to this hospital when she was twenty-one, the same age as Diane, and she died on the operating table. I planted a rose for her, over there in the corner. You can't see it, too many others have been planted there now.'

I couldn't make out his features, only the outline of his long, bearded face and the pale whites of his eyes. 'I thought . . .'

he said after a long pause, and his voice shook, 'I thought perhaps she had spoken.' I didn't understand at first. But slowly it dawned on me that he had come into the garden to wait too, though what we were waiting for were two very different things. He laid the shrivelled flowers in my lap and stood up. I watched him move off, his hands dangling uselessly by his side. I didn't try to stop him this time. A moment later the shadows had swallowed him up.

Some time later, I can't say how long it was, I noticed that I was shivering. I had on only a thin jacket over my blouse. I got up stiffly from the bench and made my way back to my office, to be there in case the professor should have anything to report. From behind my desk I watched the door. The minutes passed, I didn't take my eye off it, but there was no knock and finally, wearily, I turned to the files on my desk, to the patients I had neglected in the interests of one who, quite unreasonably, had taken over my life. A tall pile had now accumulated over the notes of the lawyer from Cardiff. After a couple of hours, with great reluctance, but no longer able to keep my eyes open, I went home.

The next morning I returned early, and perhaps it was my imagination, but there seemed to be a subdued atmosphere in the hospital that day. The doctors and nurses spoke in whispers as they crossed the echoing entrance hall and went on their way, their eyes respectfully lowered. I watched them curiously. These people were used to death, they confronted it every day. There was no reason why a single patient should be singled out to become the beneficiary of their grief, certainly not one who had for so long been forgotten by the world. I thought again that if Diane were to rise from her bed, Lazarus-like, and walk out into the city in which she was born, she wouldn't know it. In the time she had been away, it had changed beyond all recognition.

The atmosphere in my rooms, too, was that of a funeral parlour. My assistants greeted me with sombre faces. Laughing, I asked them what was the matter with everyone. 'Haven't you seen the memo?' one of them replied, opening his eyes wide. 'The hospital is to close.'

The patients and staff would be moving to a new hospital in the same part of the city as soon as its construction was completed, he went on, by way of explanation. Once the old building was empty, it would be razed to the ground to make way for something new. I stared at him in silence. In a way I wasn't surprised, it was inevitable that one day this place would cease to exist, that it would be judged obsolete in the modern age, and yet it had never occurred to me that day would arrive in my lifetime. I had always dreamed of working here, in this building. My life was bound up with its very fabric, the way it was laid out, the endless corridors, the segregated wards, the little chapel, set apart, even the rambling basement and its defunct computer system. I had grown used to it, and it was quite inconceivable to me that I would ever work anywhere else.

I turned on my heel and went into my room, closing the door on my assistant and on the hospital that seemed to be sporting a black armband that day. I worked without a break until ten, energetically attacking the pile on my desk, grateful for the distraction. When I glanced up at a sound it was

Mezzanotte who stood in the doorway. My heart leapt, then steadied itself. One glance was enough to tell me that the news was not good. He half sat, half fell into a chair and closed his eyes. His complexion was ashen. I waited for him to speak.

'I've been coming to the hospital for a fortnight now,' he began. 'Morning and evening I repeat the exercises you taught me . . . I've done my best, but I can't go on.' He turned his head to the side, coughed discreetly behind his hand and leaned forward, fixing me with an earnest look. 'There's a smell about her, have you noticed? If you get up close, it's not unpleasant, but . . .'

He shook his head, puzzled, and I lowered my eyes. Then, in a voice almost slurring with fatigue, he started to tell me what had happened the previous evening. Until then, he said, he had managed to remain positive, but that evening, his heart hadn't been in it; he couldn't keep up the charade. He may simply have been tired, but when he thought about the beautiful girl in the bed and the futility of his attempts to save her, despair crept up on him. It seemed to him that his whole life had been steering him towards this moment, to this patient; that this was the one task he must not fail, and yet fail it he would.

He broke off speaking to cough again. I got up and walked over to a little table where I kept a carafe of water and some glasses. I handed him a glass and he drank.

He resumed the tale of his previous evening's visit. His sense of despair was acute, it threatened to overwhelm him. He told himself he mustn't show it; that at all costs he must keep talking, must sound bright and cheerful. But what was there to say? In the end, because it was the subject he knew best, he talked about himself. He told her all the high points in his long career, he boasted a little, described the ambitions he had yet to fulfil, the prizes – both real and metaphorical – he still coveted. He had never spoken to anyone so frankly and openly as he had to her, and she a complete stranger to him. The trouble was, as he talked, the words sounded increasingly hollow in his ears. In the end he gave up, and rather than have to look at her in gloomy silence, he went to the window and unfastened the latch.

It was dusk. The smell of new-mown grass and the delicate perfume of flowers rose up to his nostrils and only intensified his grief. When he looked down, he thought he saw two people sitting on a bench: a pair of lovers. Think of that, lovers in a hospital garden, surrounded by the dying and the infirm. He wasn't superstitious, but he had been given a Catholic upbringing; as a child he had learned certain ways of looking at the world that he hadn't altogether shrugged off, and the sight of those two sitting there struck him as a sign: outside that window life was beginning again. He felt a tightening of his ribcage. He stood there, his shirtsleeves rolled to the elbow, his chest heaving with dry sobs. With great difficulty he composed himself, finished the lesson and fled the hospital. He forgot his coat, he left it behind. It was chilly that night and he couldn't find a taxi. He must have caught cold while walking home (he gave another short, rasping cough).

When he returned to the room in the morning, he went on, he found Denise Wraith barring his way. She wouldn't let him cross the threshold. He had the impression that she had arrived sometime in the night, fallen asleep in the rocking chair and only recently woken up. It was as if she were still dreaming, she spoke to him so stiffly, like a robot. The poor woman was clearly worn out. Her face was wan, her eyes didn't quite meet his, and when he tried to reason with her she didn't seem to hear him. At first he couldn't make sense of what she was saying, only that she was in a cold fury about something, but eventually a glimmer of comprehension reached him and he grasped what was bothering her.

He paused, his eyes shrank and grew like an owl's, he raised his palms to the ceiling and after a dramatic pause, said quietly: 'I left the window open and a fly got in.'

The window had not been opened in ten years, expressly to exclude flies and their dangerous dirt – but also because, as we know, temperature and airflow were carefully controlled on the wards. Now, according to Denise Wraith, he had ruined everything. A fly or flies had got in, had landed who knew how many times on her daughter's face, on her eyelids, and meeting no resistance there, had crawled the length of the eyelashes and dropped on to the eyeball itself, leaving behind it a criss-cross pattern of bacteria. The germ of infection. The fly had landed on her lips and moved inwards to her teeth, her tongue, the mucous membranes that protect the human orifices. Perhaps she had opened her mouth in an involuntary gesture and swallowed one, wings and all? Her diabetes made her vulnerable to infection and this was clearly stated in her notes. Yet in opening the window the professor had flagrantly ignored it, and now she was soiled, contaminated. Was he a murderer too?

Once he'd got over the shock of this outburst, he drew himself up in front of her. He intended to defend himself, but at the last minute the will deserted him. 'My dear Mrs Wraith,' he said, 'you leave me no choice but to offer you my resignation. My conscience no longer permits me to subject your daughter – or you – to these torments.' And with that, he turned and walked away.

There was silence in the room. 'It's all over,' he murmured. 'Nothing left.' I stared at him as he bowed his head and coughed, delicately, into his fist.

21

I passed through the great portal, circumnavigated the square, entered the tunnel to the outside world and emerged on the busy street. I passed the flower shop where John Wraith had once exchanged lilies for winter roses, the ordinary-looking house where the first anaesthetic had been delivered, the library with its domed roof and the wrought-iron gates guarding the entrance to the university. I kept walking until I came to a large square where young people, students, were milling about in the sunshine. I wove my way through them until I came to the far side of the square, where I halted in front of a sunlit, sandstone wall. It was alive with the flickering shadows of a mass of tiny birds – swallows, perhaps, or swifts. I twisted round to follow them across the sky and, to my disappointment, saw a flock of pigeons land in a squabbling mass on the crumb-strewn steps of the church opposite.

I walked on. I quickly fell into the rhythm of my stride, enjoying the sense of distance growing between me and the hospital. It was a mild spring day. Little white clouds tumbled through the sky, chased along, like me, by a light breeze. When

I saw a sign indicating a railway station, I made that my destination. I marched up to the ticket counter and bought a ticket. Then I settled into a waiting train and fell asleep.

The train was pulling into a suburban station when I woke. I stepped down on to the deserted platform and walked out of the station beneath a girl who sat like a painting behind a glass pane, her chin on her hand, the clouds reflected in the glass racing across her face. On the pavement in front of the station I stopped and looked up at the hill that rose steeply in front of me, then set off across the street, passing under an arch that marked the entrance to the cemetery. A little distance off the path, which wove up towards the summit, an old man wandered among the graves. He would walk a few paces, encounter a stone blocking his path, spin round and move off in another direction, waving his white stick in front of him. In this way he ricocheted off the headstones, trapped between them, covering and re-covering the same crowded little patch of graveyard.

I watched him for a moment, then stepped off the path and made my way towards him. As I came close I recognised John Wraith, but he was utterly changed, a ghost of his former self. The apparition wore a brown mac over a grubby white vest; a black beret capped his unruly, yellow-white hair, which now grew down over his shoulders. His cheeks were hollow and a week's worth of beard covered his jaw. Several long pieces of thread emerged from his pocket and looped and bucked in the breeze, which blew his crumpled coat-tails out behind him. He stumbled and I caught his elbow.

'What are you looking for?' I asked.

'A butterfly,' he replied, smiling ecstatically, his bluish-white eyes weeping in the breeze.

I led him back to the path and arm in arm we made our way up the windy hillside. He was thin, light on my arm. I remarked that I hadn't seen him for some time, and he replied that he had broken his shackles. He was a man without a roof, without a family, a pilgrim in the world but one with a specific quest. Something in his mind's eye – one day a small fern in the forest, the next day a butterfly – led him onwards, and it was his duty to find it, because where it was would be his final resting place. Raising the point of his stick to the sky, he declaimed in a trembling voice, 'A dainty butterfly fluttering without a care around the flame of life, and so destroying and burning her wings before her time.'

It sounded like a quotation and I asked him where it came from, but he couldn't say. A sob escaped him, as if he had only just realised that its source was lost to him forever. We were nearing the summit and I steered him gently off the path again. When I came to a halt he stopped obediently beside me, and when I touched his arm and stepped away from him, he clasped his hands on top of his stick and tipped his sorrowful eyes towards the earth.

The spot where we stood lay right up in the top corner of the graveyard, just inside the perimeter wall. The wind blew constantly up there, but the grave in front of which I stood was sheltered by the branches of an old oak tree. The gnarled trunk thrust up into the sky on the far side of the wall, its roots lay exposed like knuckles on either side of the grave, and its branches with their luxuriant covering of new green leaves swayed low over the stone that marked it.

'Who's there?' asked the old man, and when I told him it was my sister he added politely, 'Good afternoon, Miss.'

My sister, I explained, had been dead nine years. The old man didn't reply, but I went on anyway, directing the words over my shoulder to where he stood. One day, I said, my sister told me about a strange thing that had happened to her: she had climbed into her car and closed the door to drive off. When the door wouldn't close, she looked down and saw that her leg was still hanging outside. 'That's not right,' she said to me, 'I should have known where my leg was.' Two months later, I buried her, my last surviving relation. Twenty-one and dead of a brain tumour.

When I turned to the old man, he wasn't there. The only sound that reached me was the whistling of the wind through the branches of the old oak and the scratching of a twig like a skeletal finger against the weathered headstone. I kneeled down on the soft grass and, on a whim, put my ear to it. Then I put my mouth to it, but the wind whipped my hair around my skull and tore the words from my lips. I raised my voice, I was wailing into the wind, but still it drowned me out, so then I planted a kiss on the soil. When I got to my feet again, I caught sight of John Wraith far below me. He had stopped on the path and seemed to be looking back over his shoulder at me. He was blind, of course, but it seemed to me at that moment that he *saw* me. We stared at each other over that great distance, where the wind ruled out any possibility of speech. Then he turned and continued down the hill. By the time I reached the station, he had gone.

22

The case I was working on recalled a famous one from the textbooks: the lady of the rings. Following a stroke and damage to the right side of her brain, the wife of a rich Austrian industrialist denied that her left hand belonged to her, along with the rings on her fingers. When the rings were moved to her right hand, she didn't hesitate to claim them as her own. My patient, too, was inclined to deny his own body parts, but on one side only. A classic case of anosagnosia, though admittedly unusual in a child. I closed the file and moved on to the next one, an intriguing case of epilepsy triggered by a certain, very expensive perfume.

I worked furiously for a couple of hours, cleared the papers from my desk and carried them through to the secretary for filing. It was only then, having restored a little more order to the world, that I felt strong enough to ascend to the fifth floor, to make my way for the last time along the corridor to the room at the very end of it, which was still – for at least another day – inhabited by Patient DL.

As the lift doors opened my eyes were greeted by a vision

in yellow: Fleur Bartholomew resting her bare elbows on the wooden top of the nurse's station, sticking her rump into the air, over which flowed generous lengths of custard-coloured material. She broke off her conversation with the male nurse, straightened up and, with a radiant smile, announced that she had just been on her way to see me. Since the hospital was to close she had decided to take her retirement, but as there was no firm date for the closure, and it depended on the builders, she had decided to set her own timetable. As soon as she had discharged her responsibilities to Patient DL she would be leaving. A keen pang of loneliness ran through me then, and a moment later I found myself engulfed in the hibiscus-scented folds of her robe. Holding me out at arm's length, she shook her head and laughed.

'What will you do?' I asked, forlornly, and she told me that she intended to move in with her son and daughter-in-law. They were well off, they could afford to make her comfortable, and besides, she had two small grandchildren to spoil. Laughing again, she sashayed past me to the lift. 'Don't tie yourself in knots,' were her last words to me, and she was still laughing and wagging her finger as the lift doors closed.

When she was gone, the nurse and I exchanged wistful glances. He called after me as I headed into the corridor, as if he had just remembered to tell me something, but I didn't hear what he said and I didn't turn back. So it was a shock to me to discover that another room had been closed off and quarantined due to infection. The door to the first room was simply closed, which was unusual in itself, but the door to the second – the one that had belonged to the young overdose victim – was closed and criss-crossed with venomous-looking yellow-and-black-striped tape. Not only that, but the other rooms I passed were empty, the patients presumably having been moved to other wards for their own well-being – those with weakened immune systems being particularly vulnerable to infection. In each room I peered into, the bed had been neatly made with clean sheets and all trace of personal belongings swept out. The notices that had been taped up outside the doors were gone too, the ones detailing various allergies and medical instructions. The cells were empty again, identical and waiting to receive the new intake of invalids.

Only Diane's room was still occupied, the hospital authorities having decided, understandably, that there was little point in moving her. Stepping into it now, it appeared to me more shrine-like than ever, in contrast to the naked, cleansed rooms I had just passed. This patient, the feathered wall and cluttered sideboard seemed to scream, will never leave. Nestor and his young assistant were there, dressed in blue overalls, dismantling the equipment that, only a few months earlier, they had nailed to the wall above her bed. Stony-faced, they loaded the grey boxes on to a trolley as I retreated to the window to observe the operation. The boy now followed his superior's example and kept his eyes downcast. Once, when I caught Nestor's glance, I saw that his eyes were red, as if he had been crying. I asked him if he had seen Denise Wraith, and he told me that after she had spent yet another night in the rocking chair, keeping her vigil, Dr Bartholomew had coaxed her away and given her a sedative. She was sleeping now, in the room nearest the nurse's station – the room whose door had been closed – so that the nurse would know the moment she woke and tried to leave.

The boy pushed the loaded trolley out first and I crossed the room quickly as Nestor made to follow him. I laid my hand on his arm and he looked up at me. 'Which ward have the other patients been moved to?' I asked him.

'Ward?' he snorted. 'They've gone to the new hospital.'

'Already?' I said, wonderingly. 'But we've only just heard the news.' So he told me what he had picked up unofficially. This hospital, the old hospital, was no longer considered safe since all three wings had now reported cases of superbug infection. So to avoid another scandal, the government had ordered construction on the new building to be completed as a matter of urgency. Extra funds had been found, new teams of builders brought in. The intensive care wards had been finished off first, and the sickest patients had already been transferred. Now the less seriously ill were being moved. It was a slow and delicate operation. Obviously some of the medical personnel were going with them, to care for them, but the non-essential staff would stay behind to keep the old place running until the last patient had gone. Then they too would be moved, floor by floor, along with any equipment that was not outdated.

Having told me all this quickly, Nestor announced that he had to keep an eye on the boy and left the room. I stood, bewildered, listening to the rhythmic squeak of one of the trolley wheels as the boy pushed it past the first turn in the corridor. By the time he reached the second the sound was no longer audible. I moved slowly round the bed and sat down in the rocking chair.

Diane's head was tipped away from me, as if she were watching the door. Gently I lifted her hand and laid it against my palm. It was soft and supple, not in spasm at all. As I stroked it, it began to stiffen. Before my eyes, the fingers began to close, but not on themselves. They curled around my index finger, gripping it like a baby grips its mother's, and then the muscles tightened still further until she had me in a vice-like grip. I stared down at our two entwined hands, and my throat tightened. Her grip relaxed and I was able to pull my finger out and stand up. I stooped and kissed her on the cheek, and then I left her without a backward glance.

23

I let myself into my flat around ten and fell into bed, but even though I was exhausted, sleep was out of the question. In the morning, Fleur Bartholomew would stand over my patient's bed for the last time and remove her feeding tube – observed, perhaps, by a representative of the court. Diane would not receive her usual insulin injection. After that it would simply be a matter of making her comfortable until all her vital signs were extinguished and the death certificate could be signed.

I tossed and turned. Just after midnight I got up and shivered at the window, looking down on to the street which was deserted under the street lamps. I believe it was the cold rather than any decision to go outside that made me throw on my clothes, but once I was dressed that seemed the obvious thing to do. The rest of my plan, unpremeditated as it was, fell into place during the short walk to the hospital.

The lights were on in Nestor's room and he was there, hunched over the tiny card table, the mammoth headphones over his ears, twiddling the knobs on the grey boxes and watching the waveform on the monitor transform itself into weird and wonderful shapes. A ribbon of smoke curled up from the cigarette he held in his right hand, and flattened out like the cap of a mushroom beneath the ceiling. A soothing, monotonous voice emanated at low volume from a radio I couldn't see. When he saw me he carefully put out the cigarette in an ashtray, removed the headphones and stood up. We looked at each other. Wordlessly, he began to load the equipment on to a trolley. One of the wheels squealed as we pushed it out into the corridor. Nestor produced a small canister from his breast pocket and stooped to oil the axle. We took the trolley up in the lift to the fifth floor. The nurse on duty didn't even raise her eyes as we passed, the oiled axle rasping now, rather than squeaking, to a gentle rhythm.

The door to the first room on the corridor was still closed, and with gestures Nestor gave me to understand that Denise Wraith was still inside, sleeping. It must have been a heavy sedative. There was a whiff of disinfectant in the corridor, which was eerie and silent now that the ventilators had been switched off and the last of the patients evacuated. The air even seemed a little cooler to me, though that wasn't possible – they couldn't have turned the thermostat down while Diane was still there. Indeed, as we approached her room it seemed to grow warmer again, as if her last breaths were heating the obsolete air – polluting it with life.

We arranged the boxes in silence, placing them on the bedside table, the bed, a chair: makeshift perches since there wasn't time to nail them to the walls. Nestor watched from a respectful distance as I hauled the patient up into a sitting position, eased the rose cap over her skull, adjusted it and tightened the vice. He waited to see that everything was in working order. Then, though I would have allowed him to stay, he slipped silently from the room. Undisturbed, I went to work.

I wasn't surprised by what happened next. On the first trial, the Pac-Man lurched towards the fruit and gobbled it up. On the second it did the same, and in the eight that followed Diane's aim didn't fail her once. That made a hit rate of 100 per cent which, by the professor's most stringent criteria, qualified her to advance to the next phase. With trembling hands, I switched programs so that the computer screen displayed two banks of letters – something I had done only once before, in rehearsal.

The cursor moved in a wobbly trajectory towards the first bank of letters, causing it to divide in two. There were several further divisions until the letter 'b' remained on the screen. Then the cursor took a more confident line to produce an 'l'. Finally the word 'blue' flickered there in green fluorescent letters, and to my eyes it was the most beautiful word in the English language. In the time it took her to complete the second word, 'sky', I could have run a lap of the hospital, including the juvenile wing and the chapel attached to the geriatrics. But I didn't move from my post or take my eyes from the screen. I sat there, dry-eyed, hardly daring to blink. When at last I turned to look at her, there she lay, pristine under her white sheet, with her glassy stare and her bitter-lemon smile. In her cheeks was a pink glow. I leaned forward, suddenly afraid that she would over-exert herself. 'Rest now, Diane,' I whispered.

My heart was beating uncomfortably fast, the palms of my hands were clammy and it did me good to walk briskly along the corridor where the air was cooler and the light dusky. Turning back again just before I reached the room in which Denise Wraith slumbered, I spared a thought for Nestor, seated in the basement in front of his own screen, seeing everything I saw; knowing, like me, what it meant and impatient to see where it would lead. As it turned out, he must have witnessed the next stage of our pupil's progress before I did, because when I returned to Diane's bedside more words were already flickering on the screen. 'Fly, lip' was there, and others were being constructed: 'flower, petal . . .' A word was begun, then abandoned. 'What month . . .' My neck prickled with surprise and pleasure as a question was addressed to me, and I responded eagerly, 'May.'

The scribe paused, as if assimilating this information. The screen a temporary void, the green cursor flashed rhythmically in its top-left corner, awaiting further instructions. I waited too, holding my breath. The next words came in a staccato burst: 'Eat vomit. Compound eye. Ugly. Ugly shirt.' The cursor blinked in the silence that followed and I blinked stupidly back at it. Was it a joke? Was she flexing her muscles, limbering up as a pianist does by playing scales? She still wore the child's blouse decorated with ladybirds, whose cuffs fell short of her wrists. Before I had time to come up with a suitable reply, another word appeared on the screen: 'Midnight'.

I glanced at my watch. It was a quarter past two. When I looked up again the word 'professor' had replaced the last, or rather embellished it, removing its ambiguity.

'Tomorrow. It's the middle of the night now, he's sleeping.'

The screen remained empty. Was she relieved, disappointed or indifferent? 'Diane?' I asked, anxiously. 'Diane?'

I reminded myself that she could be drifting in and out of consciousness; that her periods of wakefulness were likely to be brief and fragmented. Outside the window it was still dark. There were no stars in the sky, and the windows on the facing side of the wing were dark too. The silence stretched out on all sides of me. I sat down in the rocking chair, pulled the pink blanket up to my shoulders and settled down to wait for my patient to speak again. It was then, I think, that I dozed off.

24

'Cool air, blue sky. I bathed my eyes in the blue. I was happy.'

I woke with a start, it took me a moment to remember where I was, and then I saw those words on the screen. Turning in amazement to my patient, I saw that her pupils were dilated, as if hungry for light, or perhaps embracing that memory of sky. More words appeared and I realised that she was thinking of the helicopter ride that had brought her to the hospital, ten years earlier. She talked about it as if it had only happened yesterday. In halting sentences she described the feeling of lightness, of liberation.

It seemed to her, she was saying, that the blue belonged to her – it was her natural medium and she felt drawn into it. Later, tearing her gaze away from it, she noticed that a body was laid out beneath her. It was wrapped in a grey blanket and the blanket was tightly secured with belts. The belts bound the arms to the body's sides. Beneath it was a stretcher, and further out she could just make out the shoes and turn-ups of two men. They occupied her peripheral vision, they sat either side of her, like guardian angels. Heads and torsos were out of sight, but her right-hand man rested a proprietorial hand on one of the body's bound arms, and this hand she studied closely. It had a thin covering of black hairs that extended down the wrist from the cuff of his shirt. The skin was yellowish, the fingernails clean but bitten down to the quick. It belonged to a young man, obviously, and with his foot laced into a desert boot this young man was impatiently tapping the floor. It amused her to watch that tapping foot. How angry he was! The other angel seemed more at ease. His green-sheathed legs were crossed at the knee, leaving one white plimsoll poised at an elegant angle in mid-air. The three of them seemed to be enclosed – save for the hatch and the sky beyond – in a sort of white cylinder. There was a smell of air in vast, rushing quantities, every now and then tainted with oil. In her head was a terrible drone, an almost deafening whirring sound, and occasionally there was a jolt, or a dip in her line of sight, which suggested to her that the cylinder was in motion. She took it all in calmly and then allowed her gaze to slip back into the soothing blue. In her mind the body raised itself up and wandered towards the hatch, from where it took flight. 'I imagined the arms pressing out on the belts, loosening them, the legs taking a running jump, the arms spreading, the body soaring . . .'

Occasionally different smells wafted up to her. Grass, trees, water – yes, she knew when they flew over a river. It was early autumn. The air was warm with pockets of cold. The journey seemed to last a long time. Then a crane bobbed into her field of vision, puncturing the blue and her euphoria with it. Tower blocks followed, church spires, tiled roofs, treetops, and finally the helicopter brought her down to earth with a bump.

I asked her if she remembered anything before the helicopter ride.

'No.'

It seemed incredible. I pushed her once or twice more for details of her former life, for memories of her childhood, but her answer was always the same: nothing.

'You were twenty-one when you came to this hospital,' I pointed out, and that seemed to capture her attention. She asked me how long she had been there. When I told her she receded into silence, and it was half an hour before I could get anything else out of her. When she signalled to me that she was ready to speak again, I asked her what else she remembered about the day she arrived at the hospital.

'To begin with I thought I had come to a prison, to a place where they tortured people,' she wrote. 'They prodded and poked me. Without warning, they would lift me on to a trolley and trundle me off into the bowels of the building. I was left in draughty corridors. Then they pushed me into small, stuffy rooms, held hypodermic needles up in front of me, squirted transparent fluid into the air. I lay in tunnels in the dark, listening to loud, machine noises. I begged them to let me out. In return I'd tell them everything they wanted to know. But they ignored me.'

Gradually she realised that it was not a prison she had come to, but a hospital. The realisation made very little difference. She gathered, from listening to the nurses, that hers was a serious case. What they said made her look at this body beneath her with more interest. Perhaps she was supposed to feel differently about it. She really couldn't muster any feelings towards it at all. It was neither a help nor a hindrance, merely a benign growth that seemed to travel with her, that seemed to be attached to her in some way – although she considered it a foreign object. The distress that she felt was not in any way connected with the body. It was due to her strange impression that she had become invisible. Neither the doctors nor the nurses ever addressed her directly, and she could not make them listen to her. She blinked at them, or rolled her eyes to get their attention, but they just smiled or looked through her. They were always in a hurry. The nights were the worst. She would lie awake, listening to the whimpering of the man in the next room. If she dozed off, he would still be whimpering when she woke up. She was helpless to exclude the sound, and the nurses did nothing about it. She felt like a child on her father's thigh, tugging at his sleeve: however hard she tugged, he never looked down.

She told me she felt a little tired and broke off. These silences, or rest periods as I came to think of them, happened quite frequently. I let her rest for a minute or two, and then I asked her if she was in pain. No, she replied, not pain. Physical pain was not something she suffered from a great deal, though she knew what it was. She was more familiar with anguish, which she considered just as bad. The worst example of this was the time when, for no good reason, this body, this normally inert appendage seemed to take on a life of its own. The growth turned malignant; it inflated. She watched it, first in wonder, then with anxiety, then in terror. To begin with she laughed it off when the nurses made cruel remarks about it; when they lifted it out of bed in a crane, a sort of canvas sling, and swabbed its fat belly and juddering thighs with flannels. Later she cursed them, and it. The body kept on growing, it began to restrict her field of vision. The belly obscured the footwear of her visitors, then their shins and their lower halves from the waist down. The rolls of fat around her eyes made it difficult to blink, let alone to look to left or right, up or down. Her window on the world shrank to a slit and then to a pinprick. She was trapped in an outsized blubber suit. Just when she was beginning to think that the growth would engulf her entirely, that she would never again look into a blue sky, the tide of fat began to recede, the body shrank back to its previous, acceptable form, and her window on the world resumed its normal proportions.

A brief silence, and the word 'Midnight' reappeared on the screen.

'In a few hours,' I said. 'First, tell me about your visitors.'

There had been many, she said, but there were three who came more often than the others. She had the impression that two of them, at least, had nothing better to do with their time. There was an old man who sat by her bed, massaging her hands. He was blind and lonely; she sensed that he had led an unhappy life. One day, to thank him, she waved her hand over her treasures, the trinkets that were arranged on her sideboard, and said, 'Please, take something. Anything.'

He stood uncertainly for a moment, then he moved slowly along it, trailing his fingertips over the objects. Cupping his hand round an apple, he lifted it out of a bowl and held it up, with a questioning expression, for her to see. She was touched by his modesty. He nodded to her in gratitude. After that, at her insistence, he always took something away with him as a reward. The woman who came later in the day, the keeper of the pencils as she called her, would then run her eye over the assembled delights and replace what was missing. It was a good system.

'Why do these two come?' I asked her. 'Who are they to you?'

A pause. The cursor flashed at the top of the screen.

'I know who they say they are,' she replied. 'It means . . . very little . . . to me.' The last words sputtered on to the screen with the motion of a car running on empty, and a moment later she was asleep.

'The young one makes me laugh,' she resumed, after a nap. 'The others don't like him, but I do. He struts about in front of the nurses, picks fights, but when he comes into the room he's as tender as anything. He calls me angel and then he slips his hand under the sheet. I wait to see what he will discover down there. He whispers to me, "Remember? Remember this?" and I concentrate hard, as hard as I can, because I don't want to disappoint him. But I don't feel a thing. I don't remember. And I wish he wouldn't look so sad.'

'You never speak to him?'

'No, not to him.'

She spoke to the old man, even though he had too many conversations going on in his head already; her small, reedy voice was drowned out in the clamour. Just occasionally, he understood her. More often, something he imagined her to have said coincided with something she had actually said. That was hardly surprising, given the laws of probability. The woman, the keeper of the pencils, preferred the sound of her own voice. She rattled on about her life, in which nothing interesting ever happened, so that Diane often drifted off during her visits and woke up to find herself alone again. The young man, Levy, was lost in his own grief, and down in the depths of his mourning he couldn't hear a thing. It was a shame, because he seemed to lead an exciting life – he was always jetting off to foreign parts – and she would have liked to ask him about his adventures.

A thought occurred to me. I went to the wall and detached the photo of the artist in her studio. This I carried back to her, raising it in front of her unfocused eyes. I asked her if she recognised anything in the photo.

'The statue,' she wrote, after a long pause. 'It seems familiar to me . . . Yes, as if I'd always known it.'

A tear formed in the corner of her eye and splashed on to her cheek. I kicked myself for showing her the picture and upsetting her like that. It turned out to be counter-productive, because after that nothing more appeared on the screen for an hour or more.

25

She was talking about the last two weeks, the ones in which Mezzanotte had presided over her training. 'I knew as soon as he arrived on the ward each day. You will laugh, but there was a vibration in the air. I felt it as soon as he stepped out of the lift, and it reminded me of something. It reminded me that there was a world beyond this room . . .'

This stirred something in my own memory, something a blind patient had once said to me. Only when it rained did he have a sense of the contours of the world. The rain turned space into sound, a different chord representing each of the three dimensions.

Diane was still talking. Her short sentences rolled down the screen quite fast now. She seemed to have tapped some inner strength, or discovered a knack to operating the professor's machine. When I thought of how much trouble I had had even displacing the line once, it was astonishing to me to see the progress she had made. I recalled what Nestor had said all those months ago, about the machine having been designed for someone who was desperate to communicate, and for whom it provided the only means of doing so.

The words were coming so fast I couldn't take my eyes off the screen or I would miss a sentence and risk losing the thread. Until Mezzanotte came along, she said, she didn't think about the world. The world for her was that room and the people and objects that passed through it. She was the presence that filled it, the god, the intelligence at its centre. The others, the old man, the woman, the boy with the beard, revolved around her like planets round the sun. That space, roughly three metres by four, was the extent, the dimensions of her mind. Her thoughts, therefore, were small and mean. True, the television brought her images and sounds, people, places, but these she regarded, like her visitors, as works of fiction. They came from an entirely separate universe that had no bearing on her life. Only Mezzanotte provided continuity, or Midnight as she liked to call him: a link with a world that hummed with life, and had to exist because he came from it and disappeared back into it. That idea, that there was a world out there from which she was excluded, always brought her very low. Mezzanotte walked the length of the corridor, sending out pulses of energy like ripples on the surface of a pond, and by the time he turned into the room she would have retreated inside herself. Huddled down deep, she would peep out at him with fearful, envious eyes. Then he would start to talk. 'He talked all the time! I sang to myself so as not to have to listen.'

Days passed and as he kept on coming, her fear turned to indifference, then to mild curiosity. When the time came for him to leave at the end of a lesson she was reluctant to let him go. Her mind would follow him for a way, just as once it had strayed beyond the helicopter hatch, though more cautiously, because by now she had become used to her little room. At first she peeked around the door frame and watched him as far as the angle in the corridor. She stretched out a toe, inched a short way along it, keeping close to the wall, then losing her nerve, sidestepped neatly into Aziz's room.

'Aziz was overjoyed to see me. He greeted me like an old friend. I sat on his bed and he poured out his woes to me. After that I went to see him every day. He liked to reminisce about the village he came from. The blue hills, the red fort, the banyan tree. The women with bells on their toes, the fearless warriors. The picture grew more and more romantic, I began to suspect he was making it up. One afternoon he went too far; he told me a great wave had struck his village and swept it away, leaving behind a sea of mud. It was the reason he and his wife had fled. That was when I told him I was bored of his stories. I left him moping and moved on. I called on the overdose boy, a real narcissus. He said he had done it to punish his mother, and he didn't think he had punished her enough. I told him he deserved a slap himself, but since he would probably enjoy it, he wouldn't get it from me. I moved on again. Each afternoon, I visited the friends I had already made and I made a new one. Gradually, a room at a time, I visited the whole ward. I never went beyond the fifth floor, I didn't like the look of the lifts, but I visited the other poor souls who, like me, had wound up there. I gave one woman the fright of her life. I appeared in front of her without warning and she shrieked at me: "Latex allergy! Latex allergy!" A real hysteric, she was. I'd recite nursery rhymes to calm her down: "Humpty Dumpty sat on a wall . . ." After a while she did. But she still shrieked at me each time I arrived in her room, so I took to calling her that, Latex Allergy. Generally speaking, though, the patients were pleased to see me. Only one ignored me altogether, the old man in the room furthest from mine. I never got a squeak out of him, but then he was half-dead already . . .'

More of the same followed, I've remembered the gist of it but forgotten the details. I do remember her telling me that the day came when she discovered she could do other things too. 'Yes, if I raised my voice, Aziz could hear me through the wall. I didn't even have to get up from my bed. When he started whimpering at night, I would yell at him to shut up and he would. I pinched a nurse when she came to draw the curtains one morning, and she winced. I snapped my fingers and the rest of them jumped to attention. They lined up in their silly uniforms. I ordered them about a bit. I demanded to speak to the person in charge. A black lady in a terrific red gown glided in, she had bells on her toes, she danced for me . . .'

It was almost 5 a.m. She had been talking in bursts for close to three hours. Her rate of production seemed to have reached a plateau, but her sentences were growing longer and more fluent. I was timing her naps and had noticed with anxiety that they were getting longer too. It was a strain, she said, in a sudden digression, to have to rally her energy, to have to direct it always in a certain direction. If she spoke for too long, a pressure built up inside her head. Her ideas themselves began to dissolve, grow faint. 'I remember blue men,' she wrote. 'Did I dream them?' I told her to go at her own pace, there was no hurry. When she rested, I rested, closing my eyes, teetering on the brink of sleep.

'One day, Midnight came and I decided to hear him out. I could hardly believe my ears. Do you know, there were actually times when he talked about himself in the third person, and times when he tried out different titles on himself? You didn't know he had ambitions to become president, did you? Though that's odd, don't you think, because we don't have a president in this country. Oh, of course, he's foreign. Anyhow, when he talked like that, I yearned to pipe up and frighten the life out of him. I tried. I used the method that had worked with Aziz, but perhaps Aziz was more sensitive, being an invalid. Midnight couldn't hear me. So then I thought of the machine. Until then I hadn't seen the point of it. I had tried your exercises, I didn't want to let you down, but frankly they wore me out. If I had practised as much as you asked me to, I wouldn't have had any energy left over to pay my visits, so I had to choose, and I preferred to be sociable. But then it became an obsession with me to shake Midnight up, and I put my nose to the grindstone. I practised with you, once or twice, but more often on my own, at night, when the ward was quiet and it was easier to concentrate. I didn't have the equipment, of course. But I would conjure up the images you had taught me. I practised until I could alter the slightest detail at will . . . the length of the whip, or the part of the lion's anatomy where it landed; the revs of the motorcycle engine, the width of the intersection. I worked hard, until I was confident that I would be able to control the machine perfectly without making a single error. Finally, the day came when I felt ready to put him in his place . . .'

She drifted off. I got up and crossed to the window. A new moon hung over the garden, but the sky itself was lightening and the outlines of trees and flowers were becoming visible. I pressed my forehead against the cool glass and stood there for a moment, my eyes closed, resting. Then with a yawn I stretched my arms, shook out my legs and returned to my seat.

'That day he came, as usual, at ten o'clock in the morning. But it was no good, there was too much commotion on the ward, it sounded as if one of the patients was leaving, not that I was paying much attention. I was too excited. So anyway, I decided to wait for the evening session. I waited all day, it was terribly hard on me, I longed for him to come early. He didn't, of course. He was a few minutes late, and he arrived unannounced. What I mean is, there was no disturbance of the air in my room. No warning, which was unusual. When he appeared in the doorway, he looked awful and I felt the pressure start to build in my head. His face was grey. His limbs seemed to weigh him down. He took off his coat and hung it on the back of the door. It seemed to cost him a huge effort. He sat down by the bed and stared at me. I stared back, willing him to hurry up and set up the equipment, but he didn't move. He just kept on staring. Then he took off his jacket, hung it over the back of the seat and rolled up his shirtsleeves. He sat there for a long time, contemplating his bare forearms, before he got to his feet. At last! I thought. He crossed over to the window and threw it open. Then he leaned out, his shoulders heaving . . .'

She drifted off. She was drifting off more often now, and for longer each time; it seemed to me that she was battling against fatigue, but I didn't have the heart to stop her.

'The next thing I knew, I was breathing in all these scents from long ago. Smells of spring. The pressure grew in my head, I thought it would explode. If I could just get up and join him at the window, I thought, the fresh air would clear it and I would feel better. I went and stood close to him, but a little way back, so as not to frighten him. I really wasn't feeling well, though, and without thinking I leaned my elbow on his shoulder and my head on my elbow. It did me good. The pressure in my head started to ease, and seeing what I had done I stepped quickly back towards the bed. A moment later he turned away from the window. He glanced at his watch, started, grabbed his jacket off the back of the chair and hurried out of the room. I ran after him, I ran all the way down the corridor, past the rooms where my friends lay, shouting for me . . . I ran past the first corner, past the second, the nurse's station (I was afraid she would try to stop me, but no), only to see the lift doors closing on him . . .'

She returned slowly to her room, but when she got there she saw that Mezzanotte had left his coat hanging on the back of the door. It struck her that he had meant her to follow him, and seizing it she ran back along the corridor, past the now silent or whimpering occupants of the other rooms, past the nurse's station and straight into a waiting lift. It was the first time she had dared venture beyond the fifth floor, and when the doors opened on the entrance hall she froze and looked around her in wonder. She had no idea the hospital was so big. The hall was all black, it seemed to be carved out of marble. She found it beautiful, and then there was the doorway that led out into the world beyond . . . She shivered with cold and excitement. Midnight stood on the threshold, she offered the coat up to him. He took it from her and put it on.

'Go back now,' he said, not unkindly, and set off down the steps. She followed him, plucking at his sleeve until he stopped and turned, stooping so that his face came close to hers. 'You won't go? Then listen,' he said, his breath escaping him in a small vapour cloud.

He explained what had happened to her, first in technical terms, then in simpler language. The upshot of it was that her body was paralysed but her imagination was free. It was because her imagination was free that she was talking to him now. Hers was a rare condition, but it was of great interest to scientists, who would like to understand it and perhaps, one day, to cure it. But she should be under no illusions: there was no cure for what she had. She would always be an invalid. Her father had gone out into the world, her mother was sick with exhaustion. It was unlikely she would ever see either of them again. Her husband had long ago abandoned her. She would die alone, forgotten, and without ever really having lived.

He straightened up and set off again. She trailed after him, not knowing what else to do. She knew that he had meant to be cruel, but she thought he had gone too far, because she *had* lived. Yes, she had lived all right. Ever since that day when he stepped out of the lift on the fifth floor, and she sensed the disturbance in the atmosphere, she had known what it meant to be alive. So she continued to follow him.

At first she walked a couple of paces behind him, she stalked him like a small, midday shadow. Then she came up abreast of him. He pretended not to notice her. They walked through the silent city streets, crossing a square with a large, dark church on one side. There was a frost that night and the pavements glittered with it. She didn't feel the cold. The sun was coming up as they passed a cemetery on a hill, and soon after that they left the city behind them and passed into the countryside. They passed fields in which tall green barley waved in the sunshine. They climbed a gentle rise and descended into a valley. They followed a river for a few hours and entered a forest. When they reached a clearing in the trees, he took off his coat and sat down amid the pine needles, his back against a log. He tipped his head back and closed his eyes. She kneeled down close to him, breathing in the heady odour of the wild garlic that grew close by.

'Why do you wear that scarf?' she asked him.

'This?' He touched the ivory silk wound around his neck. 'Because underneath it is an old man's neck. You see how vain I am. It was an old man's neck even when I was young. But now that I'm old, perhaps I have the neck that I deserve.' He unwound the scarf and handed it to her. She tied it round her waist.

'Why do you hate me?' she asked.

Tipping his head back again, so that the greenish light cast by the canopy showed up the lines on his forehead, and the ones that ran down from his eyes, he laughed. 'I don't hate you. How could I hate you? You're Patient DL!' Throwing her a shrewd glance, he added, 'Love, hate, those are things we feel here.' He struck his own abdomen with his fist. 'You, my dear, have no right to speak about them.'

She threw her shoulders back defiantly. 'Well, in my case, I feel it here,' she said, and tapped her temple. 'It's true, sometimes I feel a sort of pressure build-up . . .'

Mezzanotte wasn't listening. Having crossed his arms over his chest, he had nodded off. Diane looked up. Above the forest canopy the sky was a limpid blue, but down among the trees dusk was gathering. She moved up close to Mezzanotte, circling his waist loosely with her arm and resting her head against his shoulder. She woke once in the night, to the sound of rustling leaves, and saw in the near distance a pair of yellow eyes staring at her. Just then she noticed that Mezzanotte had turned towards her in his sleep, bending his knees and resting his hand lightly on her thigh. An owl called. She twisted her head to look at the sky above, which was now a luminous midnight blue punctured with stars. 'Shhh . . .' she whispered to the yellow eyes, which blinked out. She let her head fall back on to Mezzanotte's shoulder, and was asleep in an instant.

When she woke the next morning Midnight was already getting to his feet. Folding his coat over his arm (the day was warm, almost like a summer's day), he smiled down at her and offered her his hand. 'It's late,' he said. 'We must go.' They walked on through the forest, arm in arm, and turned on to a white, dusty road. Very soon, they passed a couple of soldiers. A couple of miles further on, they stopped at a roadside hotel to quench their thirst. Levy sat at one end of the bar, he was drunk. Midnight spoke to him, but he looked at him with dim, uncomprehending eyes. He mumbled about someone who was lost. Wallowing in his own grief, he was as oblivious to her as ever.

They emptied their glasses and moved on. There were more soldiers coming towards them, they passed a tank and an ambulance with a red cross painted on the side. Up ahead a crowd of people blocked the road. Mezzanotte told her they were refugees from the East. Just beyond them was the border, and once they had crossed that they would be into the country of his origin. Everyone knew him there. They would be fed and offered beds in all of the houses that harboured his paintings, those paintings he had collected over the years, the fruits of his labour, which circulated the world on permanent loan. Once they were rested, their real work would begin.

They walked on. Some of the refugees were squatting by the side of the road, they seemed exhausted. Others were standing, conferring among themselves or smoking with the soldiers. The midday sun beat down on them. She looked down at a little dark-haired boy in dungarees. He had a dirty face and he was playing in the dust. When she looked up again, Mezzanotte was gone. She spun round, she pushed through the crowd, she couldn't find him. When she asked a soldier if he had seen a man of his description, he pointed to a tent a little further down the road towards the border and suggested she go and look for him among the photographs of missing persons. She didn't go, but waited where she had last seen him, squatting like the others by the side of the road. A lorry arrived and more refugees were unloaded. The crowd swelled. The air began to cool, evening was approaching and she realised she wouldn't find him before nightfall. So she turned back. She returned the way they had come, via the forest and the river. She wasn't worried, she knew that he would retrace his steps when he realised she was no longer by his side. As she walked, she got to thinking. As soon as she reached the hospital she would get started on her real work. They had discussed it during their journey. She would keep practising with the machine, so as not to lose her hard-won skills, and so that when he returned he would see that his experiment had succeeded after all. He would become even more famous than he was already. She would become his greatest success, the glorious climax of his career, the spur that propelled him into the presidency. She would be his gift to medicine and to humanity. He would be grateful to her, and her life, then, would have been worthwhile.

A pause. I waited, listening. Dawn was breaking slowly beyond the window. The hospital was quiet. The screen once more exploded into life.

'Midnight.'

I looked down at her. The early-morning light, entering through the window behind me, gilded the soft down on her cheek and her eyelashes. Her skin seemed whiter than usual, her dark eyes clearer. She looked so peaceful, as if she were once again gazing into the blue beyond the hatch, in that brief interlude before the helicopter brought her down to earth. Down in the depths of her eyes, a fire burned.

'Soon,' I said. 'He'll be here very soon now.'

She had nothing more to say after that. I called her name, softly, once. No response. Birds sang in the garden, the day had begun. I settled back in the rocking chair and turned my gaze on the door, waiting to see who would appear there first, prepared to defend my patient with my life, if necessary. Yes, with my life. But sleep was more powerful than my good intentions. And once again, I'm ashamed to say, my eyelids grew heavy and I nodded off.

26

I woke at seven in a strange state of excitement. I suddenly knew I couldn't stay in the room, waiting for fate to step in over the threshold. I had to go out to meet it, to call off the execution. Hurriedly I got to my feet, telling Diane the time had come for me to go down and fetch Mezzanotte. We would be back soon, the two of us, and in the meantime she should save her strength. She didn't reply. Perhaps she, too, was sleeping, worn out by her efforts.

On my way down to my office it occurred to me that I was about to bring news of the night's extraordinary events to the world. For a few minutes longer, that knowledge would be mine and mine alone, and I revelled in it. First I would tell Mezzanotte. To begin with, perhaps, he wouldn't believe me. He had worked so hard towards the same prize, in vain. It didn't matter. Very soon he would realise what it all meant. He was vindicated. His hard work had paid off and his position in the pantheon of great scientists assured. Not only that, but in Diane he would find answers to the questions that had obsessed him for years. Yes, at that moment, I had the exhilarating feeling that I had unlocked a secret, that I knew something the professor didn't. How much a person perceives of the world is determined by the extent to which she can act on it. A woman who was paralysed had learned to live in her imagination. With only the scantest detail to feed it – the people who passed through her room, the images that flitted over her television screen – she had built her own world, through which she moved freely. For a moment, while she had been telling me of her adventures with Mezzanotte, I had felt a twinge of jealousy. Yes, really, I was jealous of her! It passed as soon as I reminded myself that it was all fantasy. And yet a trace of envy remained, because for her, anything was possible.

The professor would hurry over to the hospital as soon as he heard, and in the meantime, I would spread the news. Next I would inform the director, who would in turn inform the courts. The decision to end Diane's life would be overturned. Would Levy be disappointed? Perhaps not. When I thought about my last meeting with him, in the garden, it occurred to me that he might even be relieved. Would he recognise his wife in her new incarnation? Doubtful. She was Mezzanotte's creature now. Her parents had receded behind her, worn out, broken, shed like an old skin along with her previous life. She would become famous, the celebrated Patient DL, described in sensational terms in the newspapers as the woman who had come back from the dead; who had spoken for the first time in ten years, and who suffered from impenetrable amnesia. Not even the faces of her mother and father stirred any memory in her, let alone the terrible accident that had condemned her to life in a glass coffin. The details of her case would be written up in textbooks and pored over by students for years to come. She would become a neurological star. From now on, she and Mezzanotte would be inextricably linked in the popular imagination. My name, too, might be mentioned in the same breath as theirs.

I entered my office, sat down at the desk and dialled Mezzanotte's home number. The phone rang for a long time before a woman answered it. She sounded quite young. A lover? A daughter? It occurred to me that either was possible, the little I knew about his private life. I felt shy. When I explained that I needed to speak urgently to the professor, there was a long pause. 'I'm sorry,' she said at last. 'The professor passed away in the night.' Silence. Was it possible? Only the previous morning, he had sat in my office and recounted the details of his final encounter with Patient DL. True, he had complained of feeling tired, and there was that troublesome cough . . . 'Are you still there?' asked the woman.

'How did it happen?'

It seemed that Mezzanotte had a hole in his heart. Nobody had suspected it, least of all him. Perhaps recent events had placed a strain on it. When he caught a chill, that was the last straw: his heart gave out. 'You were a friend?' the woman asked. 'A colleague? Well, I can tell you that it was quite sudden. He didn't suffer.'

I put the receiver down slowly and sat staring at the certificates on the wall opposite. One of them had slipped inside its frame, I noticed. I rose from my desk and made my way up to the third floor. The lighting was low in the corridors, the air icy. I passed the operating theatres, still cordoned off. The sign with Fleur Bartholomew's name on it had already been removed from her door, leaving only the scars of the tacks in the painted wood. I moved on, passing down one deserted corridor, then another. Perhaps it was too early, the director wouldn't be at her desk yet. In that case I would wait. But none of the doors I passed had the word 'Director' marked on it, so who was I supposed to address myself to? I stopped and covered my face with my hands, feeling panic rise in me. Then it dawned on me: if the director wasn't there to call off the execution, then neither were the doctors who were to administer it. Fleur was gone and the floor was deathly quiet. Nobody seemed to have turned up for work that day.

Arriving back at the lifts, it occurred to me that the temperature had dropped another degree or two in only the ten minutes since I had set off on my circuit of the floor. I pressed the button to call the lift and listened for the mechanical jolt that meant it had been galvanised into action. Silence. It must have been occupied on another floor. I hugged myself, stamped my feet and headed for the stairs. When I reached the basement, I saw from a long way off that Nestor's door was closed and there was no light beneath it. A horrible fear gripped me: that he had gone, who knew where, and taken the equipment with him. Then there would be no record of my conversation with Diane, no proof that she had ever uttered a word. I ran towards the room, almost tripping over a wire that had strayed from one of the flawed computers, but the door was locked and there was no answer to my frantic knocking.

I stood there for a moment, thinking hard. Of course, the

chaplain! He had always wanted to be useful to me, and at last he could. But when I reached the chapel I found that locked too. He had gone, following his flock. Glancing at my watch, I saw that it was seven thirty. Half an hour had passed since I had left Diane. I ran back the way I had come. Now there was only one idea in my mind: to return to the fifth floor, to the one small corner of it where there was still light and warmth.

The nurse's station was deserted. I ran along the corridor, past the first corner, the second, and froze on the threshold of the last room. The bed was empty and a nurse was making it up with fresh sheets, folding them expertly into hospital corners. Otherwise the room was identical: the sideboard still groaned under its weight of trinkets, the breeze from the open window fluttered the dog-eared photographs on the wall, the television broadcast news of our troops arriving home to a warm welcome. Only the patient was missing, the woman who had occupied that room for ten years and who had now vanished as suddenly as she had arrived.

The nurse looked up. She had a Slav face: high, flat cheek-bones and slanting blue eyes. I had never seen her before. When I asked her where the patient was, she cocked her head and looked at me with a puzzled expression.

I jabbed my finger at the bed. 'Where is she?' I demanded, hearing a note of hysteria creep into my voice.

She shook her head. Then, pulling a piece of paper out of her pocket, she unfolded it and came around the bed to hand it to me. It took me a moment to grasp what was written there. Gradually I understood that it was a memo, signed by the director. It was addressed to all second-floor staff in the north wing, and it informed them that on such-and-such date, actually that very day, all personnel would be moving to offices at the new site. These were more spacious and modern than those we were used to, and she hoped we would be happy in our new home, which would also be the country's first paperless hospital.

'I won't go,' I muttered. 'Not without my patient.'

I looked up. The nurse was removing ornaments from the sideboard, wrapping them in newspaper and packing them carefully into a wooden crate on the floor. I hurried round to wrest the paperweight from her hand. I tried to explain that the patient who had occupied this room was a special case, that she was not supposed to be moved, that there had been a mistake. She shook her head again, and at that moment I happened to glance down. I saw that the crate at her feet had a shipment label pasted on its side. An address was written on it: the number of a room on the nineteenth floor of the new hospital. I pressed the paperweight into the astonished nurse's hand, dropped the memo on the floor in a crumpled ball and flew out of the room.

27

The new hospital was magnificent: modest by comparison with some of the eccentric designs going up all over the city, but a swaggering, grandiose monument to medicine all the same. It rose from a muddy construction site, a vast obelisk covered in slabs of pink Carrara marble which, a plaque informed me, had been donated by a grateful patient of the old hospital. Sliding doors of plate glass parted as I stepped up to them and I entered a fern-filled atrium with a fountain at its centre. The air was cool and music could be heard faintly over the soft splash of water.

A giant digitised board informed me that there were nineteen floors in all. The lift glided soundlessly upwards and delivered me into a foyer bound by windows from ceiling to floor. There was a smell of new paint and recently laid carpets. I walked down a short passage, past packing crates and empty trolleys, to the point where the passage opened out into a large, circular space. At the centre of this space stood the charge nurse's station, equipped with various computer monitors and illuminated control panels. It was more like the cockpit of a jumbo jet than any nurse's station I was used to. A dozen rooms opened off this circular space, some of which already had instructions tacked up beside the door: 'Latex allergy', 'Do not enter without gloves or apron'. It was a clever arrangement. The nurse had only to stand at her post and turn to be able to see into each room, which meant that she could keep an eye on all her patients from a single vantage point. It reminded me of the chapel in the old hospital.

This area was a scene of bustling activity. Porters were moving equipment into place, overseen by the charge nurse. She glanced up from her clipboard, and when I told her who I was looking for, she pointed to a door at the opposite point of the compass to where we were standing. Then she forgot about me and went back to directing operations. A porter almost ran over my toes with his trolley, I stepped back against the wall just in time to get out of his way. I felt out of place there, invisible, and the unthinkable crossed my mind: perhaps there wouldn't be a place for me in this new hospital. It was an absurd idea, of course. My skills were still relevant, even if one day they would become obsolete, even if my props – my picture cards and flashlights, my building blocks and tuning forks, the Mind-Reading Device itself – would be depicted in stained-glass windows over the entrances to the hospitals of the future.

A little fearfully, I stepped away from the wall and bent my footsteps towards the room the nurse had indicated. Pausing on the threshold, my first impression was of the dazzling whiteness of the room. There was no clutter, not a single photograph, paperweight or vase of flowers in sight. Beyond the large window, which was double-glazed and hermetically sealed, only blue sky was visible. Patient DL lay on her back, neatly covered with a white sheet. Her eyes slid over the white ceiling; on her lips was a bitter smile. There was not a single worry line on her face, nor silver hair among the chestnut locks that curled against the pillowcase. She looked as child-like and serene as on the day I met her, and as I gazed at her, it seemed to me as if the last three months had never happened, as if the professor's scheme had never advanced beyond a thought experiment, which had died with him. There would be other experiments in future, and some of them might even succeed. But there would always be a Patient DL, lying in a room on the top floor of a hospital, trapped between life and death, forgotten, until the day came when the world would once more turn its puzzled gaze on her. She it was who marked the centre, and who would light my way back there when I got lost. As long as there was Patient DL, then I was needed.

I stepped up to the bed. As I did so, the corners of her mouth twitched out into a smile of pure joy. I sank down on to a chair that had been placed by the side of the bed, stretched my arms across her in the closest thing I could manage to an embrace, and laid my head gently on her shoulder.